THE CURE

BY JEREMY P. HORGAN

To Nigel
I Hope You Find 'The Cure'
Best Wishes

Dedicated to The Survivors, The Warriors and The Angels

CHAPTER ONE

'I can remember my father telling me bedtime stories when I was a young girl. Stories about a time where people lived their lives carefree and happy. Life wasn't perfect, but people made the best of it. He would tell me of times when he and my mother would meet friends for social events, lavish dinners and cocktail parties. Then times he would tell me of when he and my mother would take long walks on the beach, stopping for ice-cream, just sitting peacefully and taking in the atmosphere. Not talking, but just feeling the rays of sunshine on their faces. The life he spoke of sounded blissful. Watching movies at the cinema with popcorn or meeting his colleagues for a drink, which turned into four or five. Sometimes simply just walking down the road and acknowledging people he passed. Then one day, everything changed.

They called it The Cure, but truthfully no-one knew what is was or why it happened. We embraced it and claimed it as a gift from God. How wrong we were. How vain of us to believe we had earned the right to treat the world as we had and be rewarded in His name. It didn't take us long to realize our mistake, but it took long enough for the damage to have already been done.

On the eve of 2021 life changed as we knew it. People who were ill or suffering from disease simply got better, from everything. Cancer, heart disease, kidney failure, even the common cold. It all just disappeared in an instance. The leading medical geniuses in the world were baffled. It was a miracle. No doubt about it.

The first few months people were skeptical and continued to worry that the disease and illness would return. But when it didn't, they rejoiced. Everyone who had been ill was cured and anyone who may have gotten ill in the future didn't.

After those few months people returned to their lives with their loved ones unaware of the consequences of The Cure. There is a Spanish phrase which was about to be more relevant than we knew, '*quitar con una mano lo que se da con la otra*', which means to give with one hand and take with the other.

We were so caught up with the gift that we were blind to what was going on in the rest of the world and the effect The Cure was having on them. Other countries were going through the same situation, praying to their different deities and thanking them for the gift that had been bestowed upon them. But unlike us they were already feeling the consequence of what was happening.

Third world countries were most affected. Imagine a world of no HIV or Malaria. Imagine five million people a year in Africa dying of hunger, not actually dying. An already huge continent of over a billion people without food, increasing in population every day, but still without food. But we still didn't see it coming.

Starvation is a deficiency in calorie intake below the level needed to maintain life. It is a form of malnutrition and in humans prolonged starvation can cause organ damage and eventually death. But in a world where organ damage is no longer an issue starvation turns human beings into something altogether different. Food is Life.

Two years after The Cure our natural resources became depleted and the army was deployed to enforce martial law to eradicate increasing crime. People stockpiled but it was too late. The increase in population and the fact people had become greedy due to no longer worrying about health risks had wiped out food sources across the whole of the United States. Shops were looted, farms destroyed, and animals hunted and killed. After five years even cannibalism became a whisper on the street, but the government were powerless by this stage and refused to acknowledge it. As money became obsolete and as food became more valuable than gold, the soldiers the existing government had deployed to the cities either left their posts and returned to their families or had banded together for their own survival. Life in the cities became survival of the strongest.

People were still dying, but not to the same extent as natural death attrition. The damage had already been done. Murder was prevalent and people disappeared never to be heard of again. We were wiping out the population through crime but with no energy source to replenish it.

Almost everyone had left their jobs and shops and stores were abandoned. Hospitals no longer existed. The Cure had put most doctors out of work, not to mention thousands of other medical support staff. A few stayed open to cater for accidents, but in time they closed too. Simply put, lives became cheap and the more people that died the better it became for everyone else. The apocalypse was coming.

Those left alive in the suburbs stayed inside other than to loot neighboring houses for food supplies. There was still a running water supply and electricity manned by technology put in place as a precaution for a major event. But when you yourself are considered food putting on a TV or lights was a sure-fire way to draw attention.

In the cities people still stayed in groups living off rodents, birds or whatever they could lay their hands on. The cockroaches always find a way to survive and so they did. People would do whatever it took to stay alive, whether it meant giving up their bodies, becoming slaves or even selling their friends and families for a can of beans, just to take away the pain.... and there was pain.

Once the mental effects of what was happening faded and the loss of loved ones had been replaced by the physical pain of not eating for weeks, or even months, these shells of former human beings became something else, something rabid. The mind still partially coherent but with only the purpose of self-survival they became feral. Their bodies looked collapsed and exhausted. They moved around the streets scavenging in packs, occasionally turning on each other. Hunting anything that moved. The physical pain of not eating made them into the worst possible monsters.

Of course, there were the few who had always harbored conspiracy theories of this very scenario and had always feared what others laughed off. They had built bunkers and began stock piling for this very moment for years. Forgiving of those who thought they were mad until the time came that they weren't. And then, and only then, locked away safely in their homes they lived hidden from the crowds living life day by day with no knowledge of what the future would bring.

Many of the rich and famous had evaded the same fate too, managing to buy their way to a haven. But for how long nobody knew. Stockpiling would have a shelf life too and eventually even those with foresight would be in the same boat, wasting away until they too would consider the unfathomable.

Then there was us, the 'lucky ones. I was the daughter of a government scientist, tasked with finding an answer to what was happening across the country. Starting as a medical researcher my father had stumbled across a potential cure to several cancers, which could have saved thousands of lives. He was brought into The White House as a consultant, but before funding had even been approved The Cure had completed his work for him. Mercifully, as a result of this we were saved the horrors of what the rest of the population were now having to endure.

The President, his confidants and many of his workforce, along with some of the world's most renown scientists, ecologists and out and out geniuses and their families had been moved to a secure location when the consequences of The Cure were known. The President remained in control of the country as much as was possible and continued to remain in contact with the outside world through televised communications. They continued to work on different ideas as to what had caused The Cure, but more importantly how we could mass produce an alternative method of food. We were losing that war too.

In 1961 the US Government had built a town on the outskirts of Big Bend National Park, Texas, far away from the next closest town or any through roads. To any passers-by it was simply a ghost town that had long been empty with nothing left behind. With no shops, no water and no people it made a good sleeping place for the night but next day any drifters had no choice but to move on. Unknown to anyone who would pass through that town, fifty feet below them was a government base, built as a disaster recovery site in case alien intelligence existed.

Twenty-four acres of bomb proof secure steel was where we lived. 2,865 of us to be exact. We were a community that had been living under the ground for over ten years. Food was rationed but we lived a healthy life with no fear of what was going on above us. We had enough food and the ability to produce more to live down here indefinitely. We had built homes, relationships and friendships, but we hadn't seen the sky in years. It was only us down here simply because our parents had been tasked with saving the world. But even the most creative minds in the world were failing to come up with a way to reverse what was happening.

Out of those 2,865 a very small proportion were children. I was 18 years old and one of the eldest of around seventy other kids on the base. My father, Ethan 'Wanikiy' was Sioux Native American but left his tribe to follow his calling as a man of medicine and had become a key scientist in the project to help the President wage war against The Cure. My mother had been a nurse and met my father through work. She had devoted her life to helping others but passed away when I was still young from a brain tumor. After that my father became obsessed, working all the hours of the day to find out if he could have prevented it. Our relationship was strained, and I rarely saw him as he was locked away in his laboratory. I knew he loved me, but part of him had disappeared after my mother died, never to return.

The kids on the base had little input or role in the prevention of the world imploding, and we took each day as it came, unaware of the reality of what was happening to people across the states and unaware of what they were becoming. Instead we lived life like nothing was unusual. Like the world wasn't imploding around us. We didn't know we had a part to play in this war and carried on life as normal. Love, laughter and happiness were possible in a successful community, because we were unaware of the seriousness of the atrocities happening in the world above us. We continued our lives as best we could, not knowing just how bad things were or choosing not to believe they could be so bad. Our parents hid the truth from us for years, but as we started to become young adults eventually we started to ask questions.

I had grown up from a very young age with all the other children on the military base and we had an extremely close connection. The president's sons, Logan and Daniel, had been my friends since the start and we became inseparable, often compared to the three musketeers but more often the three stooges. They were there for me and helped support me in any way they could. Logan was strong, physically and mentally, and as soon as he was old enough he asked his father to join the army on the base as his security detail. Daniel however was a dreamer. Daniel was three years younger than Logan and the same age as me. He was my closest friend and we would stay awake at night talking about what might have been if The Cure hadn't brought us to this place. He was physically his brothers equal, but emotionally he couldn't process the fact that he knew people were suffering when we were not.

Logan would gather the kids old enough to understand what was happening on a daily basis. He would give them information as to what was happening on the outside of the base, and how the '*people in charge*' were looking to make everything right again, so America could rise like a Phoenix from the ashes. Logan was clever in that he only ever told them enough to stay positive and continue living the way we were, without worry or stress. But Daniel knew his brother and he knew he was holding back. Things were a lot worse than we could even imagine.

The brothers loved each other but as time went on Daniel distanced himself from both Logan and me and Logan saw this as his opportunity to tell me how he really felt about me. So began a love story in the worst of circumstances. Little did we know that everything was about to change again, as The President was about to make a decision which would affect the whole of the country.

And as for me, well, my name is Tallulah Wanikiy.'

CHAPTER TWO

'Tals. You coming over tonight?' a girl shouted across the canteen to Tallulah.

'I'll see what I can do Faye. Dad will no doubt be working late. I'm normally asleep by the time he gets back home and he's gone when I wake up,' she replied.

The girl approached Tallulah 'Tell him Tals. He needs to be there for you too. He's your father and he has a responsibility to you as well as the people on this base. You're his daughter.'

'Yeah, but it's tough when he's the one trying to save the world. I get it. It's fine,' said Tallulah.

'Mm, well I'm trying to save the world, one boy at a time,' she grinned 'and talking of boys,' she raised her eyebrows as a young soldier threw his arm over Tallulah's soldier.

'Logan,' Faye said. 'Can I steal her tonight, or you got plans to wine and dine her?'

'All yours tonight I'm afraid. Big meeting this afternoon. Not sure what it's about but it sounds serious. All the top guns are going to be there,' said Logan.

'Your loss is my gain. Hey, where's that brother of yours. Tell him I was looking for him,' she winked at Logan 'See you at eighteen hundred hours Tals,' she saluted, mocking Logan, and walked away smiling.

'Sir yes Sir,' she replied.

'Very funny. You eaten lunch yet? I've got a surprise for you,' he said.

'Oooh, sounds exciting. Come on then soldier, where are we going?'

Logan took her hand and they walked down busy corridors, greeting people on the way. 'Not much further,' he said to her. They reached a storeroom which had a sign on it. **Cleaning Supplies**. Logan bowed and held his hand out beckoning her to walk through the door.

'How romantic Logan. You've taken me to a cleaning supply storeroom. Are we going to go crazy and sweep out the mess hall? Or maybe even the latrines,' she laughed.

'Just look, would you?' he said.

Tallulah opened the door and covered her mouth to stifle a gasp.

The room was completely covered in fairy lights and in the middle of the room was a table covered in a red tablecloth set out with plates, cutlery, and two glasses.

Tallulah touched a plate 'China?' she asked.

'Only the best,' he replied.

Tallulah hadn't noticed a boy stood by the door as she came in and jumped as he stepped forward, arm out with a cloth over it and pulled out a seat for her.

'Chuck,' she giggled 'He put you up to this?' she smiled.

'Madame,' the boy said, pushing the chair in behind her.

'This is amazing,' she said. 'You did all this for me?'

'Of course, who else?' Logan sat down and took one of her hands in his.

Chuck stepped away and removed a bowl from one of the shelves in the room and placed it in the middle of the table. Then took a small jug and placed it down beside the bowl.

'Thanks Chuck,' said Logan 'I think we're good.' He shook Chuck's hand and Chuck left the room grinning from ear to ear.

'Oh, My Goodness. Is that what I think it is? Strawberries! Where did you get strawberries? I haven't seen a strawberry in forever. Perhaps when I was three. What? Where?' she stammered.

'Let's just say I called in a favor, or five,' said Logan, taking a strawberry from the bowl and holding it up to her lips. 'Got cream too if you want it.'

'Logan Mathers you have outdone yourself,' she said standing up and walking round to sit on his lap. She bit into the strawberry and closed her eyes. At that moment she was no longer in a storeroom but in a field, sat on a blanket, the sun beating down on her face. The green of the grass reflected the sun and the flowers around them danced in the breeze. The hum of wildlife around them as she gazed into Logan's eyes and kissed him, the taste of strawberry still on her lips.

'I love you Tallulah,' Logan said to her holding her gaze.

'I love you too,' she replied.

As they were enjoying the moment, they heard shouting from outside the room and some commotion from down the corridor. 'Hold that thought,' Logan said, standing up and peering around the corner. He shook his head, turned to Tallulah and put his finger and thumb to his head. 'Here we go,' he said out loud to himself.

A boy stumbled into the room, knocking over a mop on his way in and slamming the door back against the wall. He was clearly drunk and had two soldiers behind him. 'I'm coming I'm coming,' he waved them away.

One of the soldiers looked at Logan pleadingly.

'It's fine. I've got it,' he said to the soldier and they both walked off.

'Ah, so this is nice,' said the boy holding up the fairy lights and throwing a strawberry into his mouth. 'So, this is what you get up to when you're not sucking up to the President.'

'Danny,' said Logan. 'To what do we owe this pleasure? I thought you were avoiding me at all costs. It's not liked the base isn't big enough.'

He walked around Logan, ignoring the fact Tallulah was even in the room. 'A picnic?' he smiled. 'I dread to think what you had to do to Brad Senior to get those strawberries.'

'Probably nothing more than you did to get your hands on that alcohol,' he sniffed the air. 'Look, do you want something or are you just here to ruin my lunch.'

'Tals, why don't you join me and the boys for a drink or two tonight. I bet Faye would come,' said Danny to Tallulah.

'I think you've had enough Danny. Come on, let's get you back to the dorm and get you a coffee,' said Tallulah.

'Enough? Yes, I've had enough. Enough of everyone treating me like an idiot,' he stumbled into a chair. 'I know what's going on. I know.' He mumbled incoherently and sat down leaning backwards in the chair. 'Yes, I know alright.' He lent back further and further until the chair overturned spilling him onto the floor.

Both Logan and Tallulah looked at each other and laughed as Danny started snoring.

'Rain check?' said Tallulah.

Logan nodded 'I remember my dad coming home and telling me that my mother was pregnant and that I was going to get a little brother who I could play with. Little did I know that sixteen years later I'd be picking him off the floor and carrying him to bed.'

'You can't choose your family Logan,' she replied. 'I know that more than most.'

Danny started making heaving noises from the floor. 'Time for me to leave,' said Tallulah smiling at Logan. 'Oh, but not without these,' she said picking the bowl and jug up. 'Thank you,' she kissed him on the cheek.

'You're welcome,' said Logan as he contemplated how he was going to lift his brother and get him back to the dormitory. 'Family,' he lamented.

****

'Thanks, little Bro,' Logan said to Danny pulling his arm over his shoulder and trying to lift him to his feet. 'I was at least hoping to get one of those strawberries,' he chuckled. Danny made a groaning noise.

'I can remember holding you in my hands when you were born. I was so happy to have a friend for life who would never let me down and would always be there for me. Someone I would always be there for. What happened? What did I do that made you feel you couldn't come to me for anything? I'm your brother, your family. I would die for you.'

They reached the dorm and Logan slumped the dead weight onto his bunk. 'I love you man, but I need you. I want back those days when you would tell me everything. Those days when Dad was working until all hours and we'd have midnight feasts, playing baseball in the hallways of the White House and losing our security detail. But when did I lose you? What did I do to you that made you feel you couldn't trust me anymore?', but Danny was unconscious.

'Maybe I should have left years ago. Given you your chance to shine. But I couldn't live without you. You kept me grounded and happy. Helped me on the days when Dad wasn't around and I needed a friend. I would do anything to have that back.'

Logan stood and started to walk away.

'I love you too man,' came a voice from the bed.

Without looking back Logan smiled and walked on.

CHAPTER THREE

The President's bunker was a war room at the deepest part of the base, fluorescent lighting buzzing above a large oak table. Computers hummed in the surrounding rooms as the President and his supporting staff took their places around the table, flanked by their assistants and security detail. Logan Mathers stood directly behind his father.

The room was imposing, as if many wars had been won here before and history seeped out of the walls, but in fact this facility had never been used before The Cure. It had sat empty apart from a skeleton staff of army employees and cleaners for many years. Now, however, it was fighting a war not against people, but against the fact we had used the worlds natural resources and we were about to lose the world altogether.

The base itself was self-sustaining and most of the people in the room were looking to see how they could roll out a similar program, quickly and on a much greater scale, with minimal employees to do so. What they were hoping for was impossible and they knew it.

Around forty people were in the room and most would get their chance to speak. Heads of different departments took their turn to talk about food, energy, military and anything that might have an impact on ensuring there was enough food available to feed the remaining population, whilst replenishing stocks and bringing back civilization. But out of everyone talking everyone only had eyes on one person, and that was the President.

'So, where do we stand with communication with other countries and what are they are doing?' he bellowed.

Up stood Franklin J Pitkin, probably the meekest looking man you'd ever seen. A man who lack of food probably wouldn't have made much of an impact to his appearance. He wore a grey three-piece suit and looked like an accountant, but had foregone the tie as clothes were now in limited supply. The sweat came off him and carried through the room so much so that the man sat next to him could almost taste the smell. As for men you wanted in the frontline Franklin was not one of them, but if he knew one thing it was communications and he ran his department well.

'We are currently still in touch with Sweden, Norway, France, Spain and of course Britain. However, over the course of the last week we have lost contact with Russia, Germany and Australia. They have chosen to stop communications and no longer work in allegiance with us. Unfortunately, to our knowledge, India and Northern Africa have lost contact and according to the Ecology Department have less than months before their supplies are fully depleted and likely a year become the population is wiped out completely.'

This news may have rocked a political cabinet had it been under different circumstances and had they not heard it all before, but these countries were just the latest in many who had already lost contact and were known to be nearing extinction. Bigger countries had already dropped off the face of the earth and in the months to come many more were expected to follow. Not one country had come up with an answer and there was no standard strategy to why those left were still there. There were of course people still scattered across the fallen countries, but with no food there was no coming back for them now. If they still had officials in place it was only a matter of time before they disappeared.

'Can we get the British Prime minister on now?'

'He's not available sir, I believe that he is currently discussing the wall between them and Scotland. They are in critical talks to ensure that the Scottish do not cross the border. Sounds like Civil War is imminent,' Franklin stammered.

'Sounds like if they have enough army resource to start a war then they are in a good position from a food perspective. What do they have in place that we've overlooked?' The President looked down his spectacles at Franklin who was backing towards his chair nervously.

'They started the process a year before us Sir, it's purely a timing issue. Our scientists put them at risk within six months to a year. They are no further along than us Sir.'

The President tutted, waved Franklin away and slammed both hands in frustration down on the large oak table. In his prime Nathanial Mathers was a force to be reckoned with. A war veteran, he was a man with huge presence who did not suffer fools gladly and whilst he appreciated everyone's input and the enormous amount of stress his workforce were under he had started to admit defeat. It was starting to show on the furrow above his brow. Nathanial had been thrown into the Presidency having been Vice-President at the start of The Cure. When the former President decided to take his own life, he was sworn in with the job of saving a sinking ship. Being the man he was, he would not shy away from the job at hand and would never let his sons see him give up on the nation he had promised to lead.

'Brad, I guess we are no further forward with regards to food,' he threw the comment out not really expecting a response.

Brad Holton was the exact opposite of his communications counterpart. If anyone had embraced the fact the base still had access to food, it was Holton. His face was flush from alcohol the night before and he maintained not two but three chins. He was not only in charge of the scientists looking to get food out into the world but looking at ways to create new sustainable foods, like supplements and replacements. He was working with the remaining NASA staff, what was left of them, to find ways to mass produce freeze dried foods that could be easily distributed to the cities. Unfortunately, every path they investigated had relied on existing produce which was something they did not have access too. But what he did have access to was the base produce and boy did he abuse that privilege. His son and wife were also on the base and like father like son, Brad Junior, did not worry where his next meal was coming from.

Holton wasn't shy or embarrassed about his weight, bearing in mind he knew first-hand what the country was going through and he cared not what the rest of the base thought of him. As far as he was concerned, he was the sole person who would solve the world's problem and he should get exactly what was coming to him. He stood to attention with his stomach resting on the table.

'Sorry Sir, yet another dead-end. We've got people working on the mass production of replacement meals around the clock. But the timelines are just too long. By the time we have the production up and running and producing the amount of food we need it'll be too late.'

The President put one hand to his head. 'Anyone?' he lamented. 'Can anyone please give me some good news. I am due to send out a communication into the cities today and I need to give them something to stop the murder, stop the crime, stop the suicides. We need to give them hope, because without hope they will give up and giving up is the one thing we cannot allow'.

Most of the delegates tried not to make eye contact by looking at their notes, but one man sat up straight in his chair tapping his finger against his nose. His pinstripe suit made him look like a second-hand car salesman, but in this room it made him look like the one person who wasn't scared of what was coming. Everything about this man said power play. 'Nathanial' he said calmly and slowly getting to his feet. He stepped out behind his chair, flanked by his security detail, following him around to the opposite side of the table. 'There may be an option available to us.

Joshua Goldsmith was the right-hand man to the former President and rumors were that he was present when the suicide occurred. He was ambitious and had hoped to take Nathanial's place, but fate had meant he had fallen into a much lower position than he would have liked as he was untrustworthy and loathed by his own party. He oozed repugnance and by his own admission he traded on it, looking like the villain of the piece he had absolutely no problem making the decisions many others shied away from. He may have been untrustworthy, but he was good at what he did, which was doing things that made problems go away, whether it be ethical or not. He never went anywhere without his shadow McGregor, an ex-marine, for fear of confrontation.

'So, Nathanial,' he said refusing to address him as President for the second time 'We have a problem and we've been looking at it the wrong way. We've always maintained that we don't have enough food to feed the population. Right? Well, what we should be thinking is that we have too many people for the food that we do have. Are you with me?'

'No, not really Goldsmith, elaborate.' The President was already having doubts of where this conversation was going.

'Well, let me bring in Professor Wanikiy. He may be able to explain a little better,' as he gestured to a soldier by the door of the room.

Wanikiy came in wearing his white protective clothing, stooped over with papers in his hand. He was the only American Indian on the base and everyone knew him. He was a genius and in charge of overseeing every scientific project that was in progress. Nathanial had put him in charge early into his presidency and Wanikiy had been at the forefront of every breakthrough they had had so far. He was the Presidents go to man and seeing him walk into the room put him at ease and put a smile on his face, holding out a hand to shake, whilst firmly gripping his arm.

'It's been too long Ethan,' said the President. 'You need to get out that laboratory from time to time. You'll be consumed if you don't. I don't know how your daughter puts up with my eldest.' He smiled again giving a backwards glance to Logan, who remained stoic and to attention.

'Nathanial,' replied Wanikiy, nodding graciously.

'Please Professor, explain what we have discussed,' Goldsmith interjected.

'So,' Wanikiy started 'As we already know, in 2021 the population of the United States was approximately 353 million, which over the next five years grew significantly to 459 million, before dropping over a further five-year period to 235 million. We can now, from satellite imaging and our best-case guesses, put the entire population somewhere in the region of just under 98 million.' He paused, whilst the room composed themselves taking in the fact that the reason for the large-scale deaths was mostly through murder or suicides. 'Now, 98 million people is still a massive population by the standards of many other countries but given the size of our country there is still untapped resources out there which are dwindling fast. However, if the population was for example around the 37 million mark within say a month from now, maybe two, we could stand a good chance of using those resources to help replenish part, if not all the country again. It wouldn't be easy, and we would need to go state to state recruiting more military and using our own resources to bring them on board. This is not an exact science, but we've been over and over the figures and the potential to start building sustainable food supplies and we feel this is our only chance of survival. If we continue on the current path and population then we fully expect to be as good as dead in under a year.'

The president waited, and the room fell silent. 'Ethan, thank you. But the problem is that we are still overpopulated and have absolutely no way to reduce the population in time. I don't see how this is even a plan.'

Wanikiy looked to Goldsmith waiting to see if he was ready to take the question. Goldsmith nodded to him to continue. 'Mr President, for the past year we have realized that there is no way to reverse The Cure and besides which we did not think it was ethical to allow people to die slow agonizing deaths through illness or now through starvation, so we have been working on something else, something different. We knew early on that the issue was population to food ratio and have been working on a method to carry a toxin through the water supply to the cities to reduce the population.'

'Wait,' the President raised his hand. 'You're talking about genocide here, correct? Let me understand this correctly. You are talking about poisoning people.'

'So that millions can survive Nathanial,' Goldsmith interjected.

The president slumped back into his seat and the rest of the room started whispering to each other, gradually increasing to arguments and then shouting.

'Stop. Stop. Stop.' The President rose to his feet again. 'Everyone stop. Sit down. Be quiet.' The room went quiet immediately. 'So, you are telling me that in less than a year we'll be dead. Everyone out there, everyone in here and for us to even have a chance of surviving and for the population to repopulate and have enough resource to live healthily, people must die?'

Wanikiy spoke up. 'With all due respect, people are dying horrific deaths out there already. They will be dead within a year. We have longer, maybe six years, which could stretch to ten, but we have no way to repopulate the town we're built under, let alone a country of our size. We are talking about the end of all human existence.'

'What if that was the plan Ethan? What if that was the whole reason for

The Cure in the first place. Look at what the world was becoming. What we had turned it into. This is just the flood that Noah withstood. Maybe we are the ones to live, maybe this is what He wanted all along,' said the President.

'But what if we had a chance and didn't take it Sir?' said Goldsmith 'What then?'

'How exactly would this even work? How would you choose who lived and who died? How would you play God with these people's lives?'

'Wanikiy?' Goldsmith held out a hand.

'It would be completely random. The toxin wouldn't hurt them, they would simply fall into a deep painless sleep and not wake up. Some people would be resistant, but we figured that it would affect 60% of the people it reached. It would be transported through the Nebraska water reservoir and therefore would hit most of the major cities. It would however not reach seven of the major states that use a different water filtration system. And of course, it would not affect our own water system for the base. Some people wouldn't drink the water, but most would. Some would figure out that the water is killing them before they drink it and therefore won't be affected. But if our figures are correct, we should be in the region of the required population within a month if we act on this now.'

'And you have the volume of the toxin and the means to transport it to the water filtration?' said the President solemnly.

'Ready to leave today Sir.'

The President looked round to his son and grimaced. As President he knew that sometimes you had to make tough decisions which involved sacrificing the few to save the many. But this was different. This was purposely killing millions of people to ensure that humanity, regardless of who was saved, survived and did they even deserve to live? Was this all just a test?

'This is not a decision we can take lightly. Please can all heads of staff and security leave the room whilst I confer with the remaining senators.' The room mumbled and those asked to leave started to stand and walk into the adjoining room watching through the glass windows as the remaining men and women looked at each other with disbelief that this is what it had come to.

Clockwise around the table each man and woman one at a time slowly raised their hands until it came to The President himself. In silence they watched as his lifted his hand before falling back into his chair defeated.

After the board meeting was done the members slowly filtered out, shocked by the decision they had just made. The only people who remained were the President, Goldsmith and the Commander General. The President was sat down slumped back in his chair dejected.

'This can't be the only option we have,' he stated.

'Sir, if there was any other option, we would have found it by now,' said Goldsmith 'These people are going to die anyway. They are going to die in the most horrible way possible. I'm not going to say that we're doing them a favor, but we're just elongating the inevitable whilst giving everyone else the strongest possible chance of coming out of this alive. At least giving them the chance to live to an age that they may have reached had The Cure never happened.'

The Commander General stood poised to speak. Normally the most outspoken person at the table and always with an opinion but now he stood there almost unable to speak.

'General, what is your take on this?' said the President valuing some sense of reason.

'Mr President Sir, it is not often that I say this, but I just don't know. I mean, we're supposed to protect the people of America, not sentence them to death, yet here I am stood here having just voted for that very scenario. The one thing I would say is that the facts don't lie and that any other option has been taken out of our hands. If I were to vote again, I would vote the same way.'

Goldsmith held his hands out as if to say he agreed.

'Kill some to save the many,' said the President.

'We've built a community here Sir, but we will run out of food eventually. I get that you are officially still the President of the United States, but you are also the leader of this community and responsible for the people on this base. There's going to be a day when the only option left to us is going above ground to scavenge for food like the rest of the people up there. If we do this now and it opens other available paths, we can look to expand what we already have and roll that out to others in time. We sit here on our hands and then that is taken away from us,' said Goldsmith.

'You're right,' said the President. 'We need to take action. It just doesn't sit right with me. We, along with the rest of the world, have suffered as a result of not acting and now we're facing the end of humanity. But taking lives to save lives, can I live with that?'

'You either live with it, or you die and humanity dies with it,' said the General.

'Okay. Put it into motion,' said the President as he stood then left the room.

The General turned to Goldsmith 'I hope you know what you're doing Goldsmith.'

'All under control General. We need to protect the community, and this is the only way,' he replied.

CHAPTER FOUR

After leaving the chamber The President went to his quarters. His room was no different to anyone else, although with the boys choosing to room in the dormitories he had more space, which only made it lonelier. He missed sitting down and eating meals at a dinner table with the boys, but more than anything he missed the conversations with his wife. Discussing what they had done in the day and leaning on her for her advice and support. One thing he knew was that she would have opposed any plan that meant the loss of human life. She was pro-life and initially when he pushed for office she had led his campaign based on a compassionate presidential election focusing on people rather than policy. He almost felt embarrassed about the decision he'd just made. Did everyone else vote the that way because he made it clear that it was them or us, or did they genuinely agree that life had to be taken to preserve life. He ran to the bathroom and was sick.

'What do I do?' he asked himself out loud. But it was already done.

Just at that point Danny walked through the door.

'Dad' he said putting a hand on his shoulder 'Who you talking to?'

'No-one son, just putting questions out there in the hope of a divine intervention.'

'You miss her?' said Danny, looking at the photograph the President had unknowingly picked off the mantlepiece.

The President went over to his bureau and pulled out a handful of photos. He never got bored of looking through these memories and they bought smiles and tears as he regaled the stories with each one.

'Ah, this one was at a congress in Washington. I had just been made Senator and Logan must have been born the following fall. There's your mum. She was beautiful. Everyone was there to see me sworn in, but they weren't looking at me, they were looking at her. She was like a shining beacon of hope for them. When I was at meetings to raise funds in gentlemen's clubs, smoking $100 cigars, she was handing out food at the soup kitchens. Whilst I was travelling to countries to meet royalty on private jets she was stood protesting immigration laws. She really was my better half. She was a magnificent woman,' he said.

'I wish I had met her,' said Danny.

'I see her in you son. Both you and Logan. Not just your looks but she is inside your heart. I could not be prouder of both of you and the decisions you make. You'll make mistakes but you know what right and what's wrong. I wish I could take credit for that but it's all you. I know I wasn't there for you, but I need you to know that I love you both and I trust you.'

'I know Dad and we love you too.'

'Please speak with your brother. You used to be so close. Family and friendship are more important than anything and I won't be here forever. You need each other,' said the President.

'It's complicated Dad,' he replied.

'It's only ever complicated when a girl is involved. Am I right?'

'Dad!' he blushed. 'Let's see those photos,' he said changing the subject.

'Oh, my goodness,' he exclaimed 'I didn't even know that was still in here. Look Danny, this is in the Whitehouse. We never got to live there but the history in that place,' he said.

'So, who is in that picture?' said Danny.

'Let's see,' he laughed 'Well, that's Goldsmith,' he said pointing to a young man with a moustache.

'Is he still wearing the same suit?' Danny said, both of them laughing.

'That's the previous President. He wasn't the most liked President that's for sure, but he got things done and he made hard decisions and I respected him for that. I can't say that he left everything perfectly for me, as you can see' pointing around the room. 'But to blame him for everything that's happened, well, no-one saw that coming.'

'That's the Commander General,' said Danny pointing to a man stood at the back of the photo.

'Yes, although he wasn't the Commander General then. The last President promoted him just before he '*stepped down*' so I kind of inherited him on my staff.'

'Who are those other men?' said Danny

'Giants of industry. Mostly CEO's of Pharmaceutical companies. That's where most of the funding came from. I couldn't even tell you their names.'

'Anyway, enough about the past, let's talk about the future,' said the President. 'Who is this girl?'

'Just another girl dad,' he replied.

'Just another girl does not leave you like a lost puppy dog. I should know. Your mother made me wait five years for our first date,' he laughed.

'What? How come?'

'We were at High School together and she was dating the captain of the football team. An absolute adonis. His name was Will Carlton. I'm not kidding, this kid looked as if he was twenty-one when he was fifteen. Your mom was smitten. She was in the cheerleading team and I was just a Chess nerd,' he chuckled. 'Will wasn't the brightest, but your mom she was something else. Not just beautiful but stunning and clever. She had ambition and she knew that although Will was going places, they weren't the same places she wanted to be. She wasn't happy being the wife of a football star, she wanted to make her own imprint on the world.'

'Wait, are we talking about Will Charlton of the Cleveland Browns?' said Danny.

'The very same,' replied his dad.

'So how did you do it Dad? How did you convince her to date you?'

'I like to think it came after the school won a debating competition. We were discussing the rights of immigrants crossing the border and the humane response to how we should accept anyone in and help them, rather than send them back. Man, I was good that day. Your mother was sat there in the front row looking up at me. I was last to go, and we were losing, badly. Seeing her face just stirred something in me. A passion. Not just for her but for what I was debating. She brought the good out in me and gave me the confidence to know what I was saying was right. Well, I bossed it right there and then. Had everyone on their feet clapping and whooping. But only one person's opinion mattered to me in that moment and she was sat down smiling that smile at me, not clapping but just smiling. It was then that I knew she was mine forever.'

'However,' he added. 'Until the day she passed, she always maintains that it wasn't that speech that got her. It was that I was the first senior to get a Dodge Challenger.'

Danny laughed and they both sat back on the sofa looking through the photos. The President felt something inside him that he hadn't felt for a long time. Happiness.

CHAPTER FIVE

Logan sat alone on his bed with his head in his hands, a million things running through his mind following the decision made by his father in the war room.

None of this seemed right to him. Playing God with other people's lives just left a sickness in the pit of his stomach. The easy option was to walk away and just go along with his father's plan, but that just wasn't him. He only believed in good and bad and his loyalties fell on only one side of that fence.

Although the board considered him an adult he still had his own room off the main kids' dormitories. All the children had grown up living in close quarters and although they would eat and spend most evening with their parents, they all slept together in the four large rooms full of bunk beds, originally built for large scale army forces. Logan, now part of the military outfit, had made the decision to remain as head of the dormitory and oversaw a group of twenty teenage boys along with his daytime security detail for The President.

They were all good lads who got on well, other than the occasional dispute, but they looked up to Logan and respected him. They were a tight unit and were supportive of each other and the other younger groups.

Logan's brother Daniel, or Danny as he was known to the other boys and girls, was part of Logan's room, but would sleep anywhere else on the base that wouldn't involve taking orders or spending time with his brother. He still loved Logan, but he didn't always see eye to eye with his conformist ideas, choosing to hang with the other boys who would steal cigarettes and alcohol from storage containers on the base.

Logan sat silently, for once in his life not knowing what he should do when Danny walked into the room and placed a hand on his shoulder. 'Heavy is the head that wears the crown brother,' he said.

'You've no idea Danny,' he replied.

'Penny for your thoughts?'

Logan sighed and looked up towards his brother, fear in his eyes, 'Danny, I know we've had our differences, but you know I love you right? You know I'm always here for you?'

'What's going on Logan? I love you too man, but I know when something serious is about to go down. When all is said and done, you're my family and whatever has happened in the past blood is thicker than water.'

'What if I told you that something is going to happen within the next fortnight that could potentially kill millions of people. Something that is taking away the choice of every human being above ground, to benefit us. Something that we are manufacturing to take away lives to save others.'

'I'd tell you we need to stop it. What is happening is happening because of something we did as a planet of fools. We blindly accepted that The Cure was something good, when every person on this planet is guilty of something. I know its bad up there. How bad I don't know, but it's the worst kind of bad. But if it wasn't meant to be, well it wouldn't have happened. We think we have it good down here but you're kidding yourself. Look around. It's a prison. The Cure was meant to wipe us out Logan and deep down you know it. We have no right to make decisions for other people without their knowledge. That's crazy. Why did you even tell me this?'

'For once in my life I disagree with a decision that dad is making, and I cannot carry that burden alone. I need you and I need you to help me do what's right Danny.'

Tallulah had been on her way to see Logan and was about five yards from his bedroom when she started to overhear the discussion between the brothers. At first, she thought it was a usual spat but soon realized that this was something much deeper. She waited by the door listening to the conversation.

Tallulah was a rose on the base. Against the grey and green military colors, she was a light beyond light. Olive skin and beautiful features she was a young lady, but as fierce as her mother had been. She could easily pass as a pageant queen but get her in the combat ring and she'd be just as happy kicking seven bells out of the boys. Something the boys would gleefully do just to spend time with the five-foot one firecracker.

She stood with her back to the wall listening to the conversation, the blood draining from her face with each word that came out of Logan's mouth. She swung round into the opening of the door and the boys both jumped. She couldn't even speak. First, she looked at Danny who just scowled and looked away and then Logan who stood, took her arm, and sat her down on the bed next to him. 'Water?' he said and poured her a glass. Her mouth was as dry as the desert. 'How much did you hear Tals?' he said. 'Enough,' she replied.

'So, what do we do?' said Logan 'We're all in this now, whether we like it or not.'

'Break it down for us Logan,' said Danny 'Explain in detail exactly what is going to happened, when and where. We need to know everything. We also need to bring more people on board that we can trust with this information. There is no way we can stop this alone.'

'Wait,' said Tallulah. 'Whose idea was this?' Logan froze just long enough for her to know the answer. 'My dad?'

'You have to understand Tals, they think what they are doing is right.'

'By murdering millions? By taking away people's choice? Their dignity?' she replied.

'How are they going to do it?' Danny interrupted.

'Tallulah's father has created an undiluted toxin which when introduced to water will poison anyone who drinks it. There is a water reservoir in Nebraska that pumps water into forty three of the fifty states like a water highway that serves those states and maintains a constant and current flow to the larger cities in those states. It was set up years ago to ensure that should we have a natural disaster one thing we would always have is water. Much like the electricity system it is run by artificial intelligence and acts as a main hub. They have already manufactured forty gallons of the toxin which by my understanding would be enough to kill the entire planet ten times over. They plan to send a small army to the water reservoir sometime within the next fortnight and introduce it to the water system. If that happens then millions will be dead within a week.'

'Goddamn,' said Danny. 'Goddamn them. It's too late then. How can we stop them?'

The three of them sat in silence looking at the floor, waiting for each other to speak. The same feelings that Logan had had were now filling the room and the thought that someone in a room hundreds of feet below the ground could make a decision that would kill millions of people left a nasty taste in their mouths. More so that their respective fathers were the ones responsible.

'Wait a minute,' said Tallulah. 'My father used to speak about a man he used to work with. Brittle. Professor Clarence Brittle. He was a genius. The only man my father ever admitted was cleverer than him.'

'How does that help us? He's not on the base and if he was what could he even do?' said Danny.

'An antidote. What we need is something that can stop the effects of the toxin.'

Logan pondered this 'but say we could find this Professor Brittle. Say he is even alive. We have no way of knowing whether he could create an antidote and no way of getting an antidote mass produced and to all the affected cities. My father is ready to put this into practice now. Today.'

'It's a long shot I know, but do you have any other ideas?' Tallulah looked despondent.

Danny shook his head and walked across the room 'we don't,' he paused 'this professor you heard your father speak of. If he is as clever as you say he is then he could make an antidote. At this time no-one knows we know what is happening, so we can work with that. But we must start now. Logan, you have access to satellite imaging, so first and foremost you need to establish the Professor is alive. If he is alive, is he even in the country.

If he isn't then we're screwed. Tallulah, you need to try and distract your father and delay them putting this plan into practice at any cost. Whatever it takes, time is of the essence. We can't do this alone and we can't let any of the adults on the base know what we are planning in case they try to stop us. I am going to get together a team of kids I trust and lead them to find this Professor and bring back an antidote.'

'Hold on Danny. You've no military training. If you can even get off this base without anyone knowing, you'll get yourself killed,' replied Logan 'Besides which I have an idea and I think you're going to like it.'

The three of them sat planning all night, whether it be logistics of whether the Professor was alive, who would lead the team and most importantly who they could trust. Tallulah pondered the many ways she could delay the toxin being transported to the water reservoir. Bearing in mind it was time sensitive to start reducing the population the toxin would be well guarded.

Danny would oversee Logan's contingency plan, whilst Logan would take a team to the location of the Professor. But as they already discussed, there was only a small chance that the Professor was even alive, let alone whether he was still the genius he once was and not a rabid animal. It was a long shot, but it was the only option they had.

****

Finding the location of the Professor turned out to be easier than they could have imagined. Although Logan had no idea what the Professor looked like, with satellite imaging he could quite easily track down anyone still alive just by their name. There were nineteen Clarence Brittle's in the United States since 1942, but across a dwindling population now only four remained alive and only one had been a Professor. The CCTV cameras were up and running in the cities and the satellite could pinpoint him using facial recognition to his exact location, but therein lay the problem. Professor Clarence Brittle was in Mississippi State Penitentiary.

The notorious Parchman Prison was Mississippi's State Penitentiary and was a maximum-security prison that was run by the prisoners. Having killed off the warden and most of the prison guards nobody got in and nobody got out. What was last known was it was one of the last standing buildings with its own self-sustaining community. Unfortunately, that community was now made up of the worse criminals known to man and was run by a man called Isaac Mendez who was serving concurrent life sentences for multiple murders. Also known as 'The Mexican Godfather', he had taken over the prison when it was decided that, with food in short supply, prisons would be the first institutions to receive rationing and then eventually left to die. Mendez had other ideas though and having overthrown the guards they had allegedly thrown a party for all the other prisoners with the guards as the main course. Isaac Mendez had moved to the top of the food chain, quite literally.

Of course, by then the government had been moved to the military base in Texas. The events in a closed off prison was of little significance to them. So, Mendez continued to run the prison and the prisoners soon fell in line, realizing that they were safer and better provided for within the prison walls. Anyone trying to break into the prison was instantly killed, whilst the only people permitted to leave the ground were Mendez's own 'death squad' who would make frequent supply runs and the rest of the prison made no complaints and asked no questions as to what it was they were eating, as long as they were eating.

How the Professor had become an inmate was a little more concerning, bearing in mind that many of the crimes the men had committed to find themselves behind these bars was of a serious nature. But he was alive and whether he knew it or not he was the potential key to survival of the remaining population. The only question Logan had to answer was how he would extract the Professor from a high security prison being guarded by hundreds of felons.

In addition to getting the Professor out of the prison there was a lot of moving parts to the plan, which if any were to break down then they would be undone. This had to go down perfectly, which meant everyone played their part and that anyone else that they brought on board to help could be trusted and up to the job.

Even getting off the base wouldn't be easy. There were three exits which were heavily guarded by most of the army presence left on the base. Only two of those exits were for transport, which narrowed the likelihood of getting away without anyone knowing. Then there was the transport itself, fuel, how long it would take to get to the prison and back again. As the planning continued, they realized that this mission was slipping out of their hands and that they weren't capable of doing this alone. They needed to bring someone on board, and they needed to do it soon.

CHAPTER SIX

Somewhere in Boston, Massachusetts circa 2028.

Frank McGregor sat at a card table in one of Boston's few remaining taverns. The lights were dimmed, and people huddled in the corners of the room avoiding eye contact drinking whatever they could get their hands on. The barman stood behind the bar occasionally spitting tobacco onto the floor, supervising McGregor and three other men playing poker.

What made this different to any other game of poker was that the stakes they were playing for were more important than money. McGregor pulled a tin of sweetcorn from his bag, placed it down in the middle of the table and whispered '*call*' to the other men playing cards.

McGregor had previously sold second-hand cars for a living but before The Cure he supplemented his income cheating at cards and conning people out of their hard-earned cash, which turned out to be a worthwhile skill to have when the world was crumbling down around you. As confidence went McGregor's was in ample supply and he could take a beating, which also came in handy. Not thickset by any means he was wiry and muscular and had been in plenty of fights. This Irishman knew how to hit back.

Another man at the table looked McGregor up and down and without saying anything threw his cards down, stood up and left the table walking past the bar and out of the back door. McGregor smiled to himself, whilst slightly turning up the corners of his cards to take another look at his '*winning hand*'.

'You're a piece of crap McGregor,' said one of the men. 'You've got nothing.'

'So, put down or shut up Richards,' said McGregor in his Irish drawl.

'Fine. I see you,' said Richards and he placed a can with the label missing down on the table.

'What the Hell is this Richards? That could be cat food for all I know,' said McGregor angrily.

'So, what if it is? You're still going to eat it right?' Richards smiled a toothy grin from ear to ear.

McGregor smiled back 'Aye. To be sure Richards, I'll let it go.'

They both looked to the man next to Richards and opposite McGregor. An absolute monster of a man, quite literally known to them as The Beast. This man never went hungry and he took whatever he wanted, whenever he wanted. He nursed a large tankard that looked like it belonged to some kind of Ogre and took a gulp which seemed to last forever.

'I'll see it.' he grunted, and he pounded down a zip lock bag of meat on the table.

Richards gagged and looked away 'What the…. What is that?'

'Let's just say it'll accompany that tin of cat food nicely,' smiled The Beast.

'Hey, it's all good guys. If you can cook it, it stays on the table,' said McGregor.

The last man at the table was Doctor Montgomery Sherman. A small bespectacled man, who had lost everything once his job became superfluous and his wife later left him. By all accounts, in his previous life, he had built up quite a substantial nest egg which his now ex-wife lived off, with the few other people who had used their money early on to stockpile food and hide away from the rest of the world. Sherman on the other hand now slept in dank stairwells stealing food wherever he could find it.

Sherman looked at the two queens and three eights in his hands knowing that no-one at this table could beat his hand, especially as he had been counting the cards since the beginning of the game. However, what he couldn't have known was that McGregor had four queens and an ace, having acquired two queens from somewhere within the right sleeve of his coat.

Sherman grinned, thinking that he would eat well tonight, unaware of McGregor's hand and casually threw a can of peaches onto the table laughing out loud. 'I see you' he sung to McGregor who was smiling back at him. This unnerved him, a lot.

Richards and The Beast looked at Sherman scowling and waited for McGregor to place his cards down. Slowly McGregor put down two queens 'Two pairs' he said. Sherman could hardly hold back his excitement, right up until McGregor put down his second pair of queens and he felt a single bead of sweat roll down his forehead. He knew McGregor had cheated, but he also knew that there was a possibility if he called him out and laid down his own cards, the other two men at the table might think it was him who cheated rather than McGregor. He didn't want to end up on the table himself. But as he looked at the tin of peaches he had placed down not two minutes ago he felt something boiling up inside of him that he couldn't repress. That food was his. He had won it fair and square. Without realizing, he raised himself to his feet and all three men were looking at him. Even stood up he was now only level with The Beast's eye line. 'He cheated!' Sherman stammered.

'What?' McGregor said, looking for all the world like his feelings had been hurt.

Sherman's cards dropped showing the full house and more importantly the third pair of queens on the table. 'What?' McGregor said again, looking at Sherman accusingly. In honesty though McGregor was just happy that no queens had turned up in the other men's hands, because at least he could spin this against Sherman.

'He cheated,' Sherman stuttered.

'What the Hell is going on here?' Richards said standing to his feet.

'That's what I'd like to know,' said McGregor.

All the time The Beast was composed looking at the cards in his hands.

'How the Hell do we have six queens on the table,' said Richards.

'He cheated. He goddamn cheated,' said Sherman.

'How do we know it wasn't you?' said McGregor smiling a sly awkward glance towards Sherman, whilst trying not to look guilty.

'I've been counting these cards since the game started,' Sherman blurted out. 'He CHEATED.' Now this caught The Beast's attention.

'You've been counting cards?' The Beast grunted. The barman reached down under the bar. 'Explain this to me again little man,' he stood up. 'You've been counting the cards?'

'Well, yes, that's not against the rules. Is it?' Sherman bravely replied.

Someone from the depths of one of the corners of the room oblivious to what was going on at the card table made their way to jukebox and gave it a kick. It stuttered, scratched and then started playing some *Cypress Hill* song.

Sherman didn't feel a thing as The Beast brought an elbow down on his jaw almost ripping it clean off. He just lay there shaking on the floor unable to speak. Richards vomited at the sight of Sherman's jaw mangled and hanging from his face and was retching uncontrollably. The Beast lifted Sherman off the floor by his shirt and threw him against the side of the bar with a sickening crunch. Sherman was still conscious and looked like a rag doll, looking up at The Beast waiting for death.

The Beast turned around to look at McGregor who was reaching for the food on the table, whilst Richards had slipped out the back door and was lent up against a wall behind the bar heaving. 'Going somewhere Irishman?' He said to McGregor.

'Just collecting my winnings Beasty.' I did win after all, regardless of that cheat over there.

'He may be a cheat Irishman, but he's a clever cheat. If he said he was counting cards, then that means you found two queens out of thin air.'

'How can you believe a man like that? He'd do anything for a square meal Beast. Look at the weasel.' Sherman was now fitting with blood and foam coming from his mouth. Without so much as a second thought The Beast brought down a size twelve boot down on Sherman killing him. 'He isn't cheating anymore.'

McGregor kept the table between himself and The Beast all the time eyeing the exits and wondering how he was going to get out of this predicament. 'OK mate, you got me,' he conceded, dropping a half dozen cards from his sleeve and laughing. The Beast grabbed the edges of the table and threw it forwards towards McGregor who easily side stepped it.

'Looks like you'll be the main course McGregor,' snarled the monster in front of him.

'You'd feed a whole town you big idiot,' McGregor shot back. At not one point did McGregor show any kind of stress or worry. In fact, he was completely in control.

McGregor moved towards The Beast, ducked under his arm and punch him in the throat. The Beast staggered backwards gasping for air, but still snarling. He composed himself and lumbered towards McGregor, who swung The Beast's massive glass straight towards his head, leaving a cut and The Beast's skull exposed. 'Ouch', McGregor mocked. 'That's going to hurt in the morning.' The Beast shook his head and seeing double swung a fist towards McGregor. Yet again, McGregor avoided any impact and with The Beast unsteady on his feet he uppercut him so violently that his teeth ripped through his bottom lip. The next flurry of punches smashed into The Beast's temple and his eyes rolled back into his head. He dropped like a tree being felled. 'The bigger they are,' McGregor mused to the patrons who were running around the bar looking to escape the skirmish. He looked towards the bar as a bullet exploded over his right ear 'What the?' The barman stood with his Winchester poised and McGregor threw himself to the floor avoiding the second shotgun blast. 'For goodness sake man. It was just a game of cards.'

McGregor made for the door between gunshot blasts and lightbulbs exploding above his head. Through the doors he looked down at the bag and smiled. He would eat well tonight.

****

A few months passed, and McGregor had decided that the cities were becoming too dangerous, even for him. He made his way through state lines and holed himself up in a ghost town in Texas. A proper cowboy town that had been vacated a long time ago. There were no people, no running water and no food. But he had enough supplies that he would have a decent roof over his head until he decided his next move.

Sat on the balcony of the town saloon he opened the tin of food with no label, from the bar brawl, and smiled to himself. *'Evaporated milk'*. He licked his lips and drank down the sugary treat. As he sat there, he heard a noise like thunder coming towards the town. He put down the tin and lifted a telescope up to his eye. A convoy of trucks were moving speedily towards the town. He quickly jumped up and ran down the stairs as the trucks and jeeps stopped in the high street. Moving downstairs, he made his way to a window and listened to what was going on outside.

'Take trucks one through ten to entrance A and the jeeps through B,' said a man in military kit to another. 'There's twelve more trucks and five armored cars to come,' said the man.

'Is that everyone?' said the other man loudly.

'Yes, Trailblazer is safe and the remainder of Operation Cure complete,' he replied, saluted and walked away.

'De Mario,' the man summoned over another soldier. 'Look, I know you don't know all these other men, but I need you to pick ten guys and give the town the once over. We cannot afford for anyone to know what's going on here, or the whole operation is blown. Just a precaution.'

McGregor stepped back from the window and looked around for somewhere to hide. The town wasn't big, and he knew he could be easily found if someone was looking hard enough. He heard the soldier De Mario shouting orders outside the window and men scrambling towards the empty shops and the saloon.

The door opened and a pasty-faced youngster, no older than 21 walked through to the bar area, rifle out in front of him. McGregor took a step back in the cupboard he had hidden in, watching the soldier through a crack in the door. After a few minutes the soldier who had been looking upstairs throughout the bedrooms came downstairs and McGregor realized that he would at some point come looking in the cupboard. Having left himself no escape route he pulled a large knife from his jeans in readiness for what might come next.

The soldier's boots clumped down the stairs and he was looking around the bar area. Only the cupboard remained unopened and the soldier's footsteps slowly moved towards McGregor. He lifted the knife.

The soldier turned the door handle and the door started to open. McGregor considered pushing the door open quickly and surprising the soldier, but then he heard a muffled shout from outside and the soldier started to walk away from the cupboard. McGregor breathed a sigh of relief and took a step towards the door to watch the soldier.

The soldier had almost reached the door of the saloon when he suddenly stopped. He felt a warmth come over his face. His hand reached for his neck gasping for breath and unsuccessfully trying to scream for help. Blood trickled down his inside of his throat choking him.

McGregor was stood behind him with his knife drawn and dripping blood onto the floor. He cushioned the soldier to the ground and placed his fingers either side of the man's nose and covered his mouth until the labored breathing had stopped completely.

McGregor then started to remove the soldier's fatigues. McGregor had had an idea that might just save his life.

CHAPTER SEVEN

Choosing a team to take to the prison to find the Professor was by no means an easy task. Most of the teenagers on the base had no experience of the outside world let alone any kind of military training, so picking kids that could hold their own in an apocalyptic world of potential monsters and cannibals was proving tough for Logan and Danny. They already had four boys on board who Danny had vouched for. Essentially, they just wanted to get outside the base and cause mayhem without their parent's watchful eyes. The Mean twins, Scott and Seth, had grown up on a farm around guns and their father was an agricultural aide to the Presidential team. With very little to keep them occupied in the past ten or so years they had been itching for something like this to happen. They were joined by Xander Carlgren and Jay Green, both of whom had influential and very rich fathers with political ties and spent most days on the base with Danny and the other boys causing mischief.

This was a start at least. Logan had chosen two other boys from the dormitory who he trusted implicitly, which were Chuck Nelson and Brad Holton whose father ran the stores. Brad Junior was a good guy, but certainly packing in the weight department. This concerned Logan as he knew he would look out of place in the city, but he felt Brad was an asset to the team. Chuck was the joker of the pack, an absolute goon, but he was a motivator and motivation was something which he was in short supply of.

Logan and Danny had bought the six boys into his room with the intention of breaking the news to them about what the President and his team were planning to do. Neither of them knew exactly how they would do this or how their newly assembled team would take it. Let alone whether they would be onboard and help to stop it.

'So,' Logan started 'you're probably wondering why we've bought you here?'

'Well it isn't a romantic dinner for two,' Chuck said pretending to be disappointed. The Mean brothers chuckled in unison, shoulders bobbing up and down while Xander looked away, more interested in the cigarette hanging out his mouth than what was happening in the room.

'I'm just going to come out and say it,' said Logan. 'The President and the members of the board are planning on killing off over half of the population outside of the base by poisoning the water supply to the cities.' Logan took a breath and looked around the room.

A couple of the boys visibly gasped, whilst Xander looked up and then shrugged.

'We need to stop them,' said Brad, barely taking in what he had been told. 'We need to tell our parents and get them to stop this. Why are they even doing this?'

'Slow your roll Cowboy,' interjected Danny. He held out a hand for Logan to continue.

'Their plan is that with half the population dead within a certain time frame they can start rolling out some of the processes we have used on the base to the remaining population. We will then have enough food and supplies to ensure the continuation of the human race.'

'Sounds like they've got a valid point to be fair,' said Seth.

'And if you were on the outside Seth? Would you want to have that choice of whether you are in the side that lives or side that dies taken out of your hands? Besides that, who are we to say that humanity should continue?' said Logan. Seth nodded 'True, very true.'

'So why can't we tell our parents? Surely, they will use common sense to stop this happening,' said Brad Junior.

'The decision has been made. Your father was in the room Brad. He voted for this along with my father, Xander's father, Tallulah's father. They are the ones that are making this happen.'

The door swung open and all the boys jumped. In walked Tallulah with Faye over to where Logan and Danny were stood.

'The point is boys, no-one on this base is a God. It's about freedom of choice. However bad it is up there at the minute those people should have the choice as to whether they live or die. No-one has the right to take that away from another human being. They don't know that this is coming, and they don't have anyone other than us to fight for them. We are the last line of defense between millions of people being murdered so that others can live.' Tallulah had made her point and Logan and Danny both looked approvingly towards her in admiration.

'Oh, and for those of you who don't know her, this is Faye. Faye and I will be joining the team.' The room went quiet, and Logan took Tallulah by the arm and pulled her to one side.

'I don't want you going,' he whispered.

'I've just given a speech about freedom of choice and you're going to stop me? I don't think so,' she spoke loud enough for the rest of the room to hear.

Logan looked up and around the room. Danny shrugged at him and smiled, knowing the decision had been made and nothing Logan was going to say would change her mind. Logan shook his head and turned back to the boys. 'So, this is Faye and Tallulah and they will be joining the team.' The boys laughed and even Logan smiled. 'This is what we're going to do.'

Logan went on to explain about the Professor, the prison and a possible antidote to the toxin. Then how the military team planned to poison the water and when and where it would happen. He went through various maps and they talked for hours about how they would get off the base and how they would get to the prison and extract the Professor.

Danny sat back quietly listening to everything going on, all the time focused on the only thing in the room that really interested him, which was Tallulah. She was beautiful and he'd loved her since the day he first laid eyes on her. Every single day he woke, he thought about the next time he would see her and what they would talk about. She was amazing in every way. Then the pain struck him that he'd never spoken up or told her how much he loved and cared for her and how when Logan had been the one to ask her out, she said yes. How he couldn't bear to be around them when they were together and had avoided the pair of them to take his mind of the feelings he had for her, unsuccessfully.

All those years they had been so close, almost inseparable, and deep down he knew that if he had made that first move on Tallulah it could be him kissing her goodnight and shaping more than just a friendship with her. The pain was unbearable for him and he carried it inside him every day, unable to escape the base and seeing them **every single day**.

Danny blanked his mind and closed his eyes trying to erase his thoughts and get back on point. His part in the plan had not been mentioned and that was how it was going to stay. As much as the team were in too deep to back out now and had to be trusted this was the one thing that Logan, Danny and Tallulah had decided to keep between themselves. Just in case they couldn't get the Professor back in time or if an antidote couldn't be produced.

'First things first, we need to get a vial of the toxin' said Logan. 'If we don't have time to bring the Professor back to the base, we need to get him to somewhere close to the prison that he can examine the toxin and made an informed decision as to whether an antidote can actually be made. Then we need to distribute it quickly and to the affected areas. The toxin takes a week to take effect, so we have less than a week to get the antidote into the major cities and back into the water supply. If that's even an option. Brad, you have access to the stores which are as close to the laboratories as we can get. We need you and Tals to work on getting in that laboratory and getting some of the toxin. Tals, you also need to work on delaying the toxin being taken to the water reservoir. Think you can do it?'

'It won't be easy, but then none of this will be. It'll only take one thing to go wrong and it's all over,' said Tallulah.

'This is an almost impossible mission Logan. It's all ifs and buts and do we really have the ability to distribute something that doesn't yet exist to dozens of cities and millions of people?' said Seth.

'If they can do it then why can't we stop it? We may be living on a base of the most knowledgeable people in the world, but we are the children of those geniuses. Where there is no light, we make light. And if we fail, then we fail trying and giving it everything,' Logan said.

'That's good enough for me Captain,' laughed Chuck.

'Me too,' said Xander. 'Anything to get off this base.'

'Good,' said Logan. 'Talking of getting off the base there are three exits in total but only two that have access points for vehicles. We will take one of the larger jeeps and that should hold the whole team. Danny will take one of the military motorbikes. These exits points are manned twenty-four seven by a minimum of two armed guards on a ten-hour rota basis. So, if we take two of those guards out at the start of their shift, we have potentially got a ten-hour head start and every minute counts. Scott and Seth, I need you to get some tranquilizer darts from the armory and we'll use these to put them out. Nobody, and I mean nobody, gets hurt.'

'So Chief, we've got a week before they set off, but you haven't told us exactly when our little plan is going to happen,' said Chuck.

Logan looked down and then back up at them 'It's happening in two days' time.'

Chuck just grinned 'Well, I'd need to check my diary, but I think it's free for the next five years so what the Hell.'

'We better get going,' said Brad looking at Tallulah, who nodded and they left the room. Logan continued to address the room while Danny stood up and followed Brad and Tallulah. He grabbed Tallulah's arm and she gestured to Brad that she'd catch up.

'I'm sorry Tals.'

'You've nothing to be sorry for Danny. I get it. You needed your space, it's fine.'

'No,' he paused. 'That's just it, I didn't. I didn't need space. I just care, ok?'

'I care too Danny. I always have and always will. You're like a brother to me.'

Danny's head dropped. That was the last thing he wanted to hear. 'Just be careful Tals.'

Back in the room everyone was talking at once about their own separate part of the plan that they would be playing in this operation. Faye and Jay Green were talking to each other whilst the Mean Twins were discussing the armory. Xander sat alone facing the wall smoking what seemed like an endless supply of cigarettes.

'Do we have a plan gentleman?' said Logan 'and lady,' he checked himself.

They all nodded and agreed to meet back at Logan's room again after light's out.

'So, Danny, just us left. Do you think you can do it?' said Logan to his brother.

'I can do it. I just keep having these doubts telling me we should just tell dad what we think. He's a reasonable man and I'm sure we can convince him to reconsider,' pleaded Danny.

'He's a reasonable man in an unreasonable time Danny. This decision wasn't his to make and had he made it alone I think you're right. But he's got Goldsmith in his ear and so have the rest of them. Goldsmith is a salesman at the end of the day. He wants this to happen and he will do everything he can to make that happen, at the expense of anyone who gets in his way.'

'OK Brother, I'm with you all the way. I always have been,' and he put a hand on his older brother's shoulder reassuringly. Any negativity and everything that had gone before was shifted in that gesture and the brothers embraced. 'Let's do this.'

In the meantime, Brad and Tallulah had reached the stores and were trying to improvise their way into the laboratory to get some of the toxin and do anything that may delay the President's plan.

Brad tapped on the glass window where his father was in deep conversation with Tallulah's father. Brad Senior beckoned them in forgetting that the door was locked by an electronic keypad. He left Wanikiy and walked over to the door, punched in some numbers to a keypad on his side of the door and warmly welcomed them both in. Whilst he was accommodating to the kids, Wanikiy looked away to his desk before looking back grimacing.

'Junior, how you doing? Nice to see you both. What brings you here? Let me guess, you want some crisps,' he smiled and rubbed his stomach, 'some chocolate perhaps?'

Brad nodded and turned to Tallulah, who was observing her father.

'Yeah, that would be great dad, thank you.'

'Come with me then son, let's see what we can do,' said Brad Senior walking towards the door.

'I'll catch you both up,' said Tallulah, pointing to her father who was now sat looking into a microscope. Both Brad Senior and Brad Junior acknowledged her and walked towards the storage area.

'Hi Dad, how are you doing?' she said to her father's back.

'I'm very busy Tallulah. What is it you want?' he replied not looking up from the microscope. Meanwhile Tallulah's eyes were scouting the room looking for something, anything, that could be the toxin or some way to disrupt her father.

'I'm just checking in Dad. You're working way too hard and we haven't even sat down together in the last month. I miss you Dad. I miss listening to your stories. I miss laughing together and reminiscing. I miss you hugging me and telling me *you're my little Kimama*. I miss it all.'

Wanikiy sat back and spun around in his chair 'Look Tallulah, I'm sorry. I'm sorry that I'm not the father I used to be. I never meant it to be this way, but then your mother was never meant to leave us. If you want someone to blame then fine, blame me, but we're here and we're alive because of your mother and what she meant to me. I loved your mother and we were meant to be together forever, but it wasn't to be. Every second I spend with you I see her, and it hurts me more than I can take. I love you and I will always love you but right now I need to work on this project for the President to make sure that in five, ten, twenty years and more that I have the opportunity to be a better father and to love you until I join your mother.'

He didn't have the chance to see a tear roll down Tallulah's cheek as he turned away and back to his work. Through the tears Tallulah spotted a fridge on the wall behind her father with several vials all marked as hazardous. She slowly backed towards the fridge whilst keeping an eye on the scientists feverishly working away in the next laboratory through the glass wall. Her hand slipped in through the fridge door and slowly and quietly removed one of the vials. The label on the vial declared Project Nebraska and Tallulah knew she had found the toxin.

Just at that moment the laboratory door opened and Goldsmith walked through the door glaring at Tallulah, swiftly followed by McGregor eyeballing her as she moved her hands behind her back.

'Ah, a Wanikiy family reunion,' he joked 'in the Presidents top secret laboratory,' the tone changed immediately to one of irritation and resentment.

'She's just leaving,' Wanikiy looked up at Goldsmith with equal distain at both the fact Tallulah was still there and that Goldsmith now stood in front of him.

'Good, good,' said Goldsmith giving Tallulah the once over and then looking away as if she didn't exist.

Wanikiy and Goldsmith despised each other with a passion. Wanikiy knew Goldsmith was a self-obsessed narcissistic bully and Goldsmith knew Wanikiy knew this and it grated on him. Even more so because Goldsmith's plan completely rested on the scientist's shoulders.

'Where are we?' Goldsmith stopped and looked round at Tallulah 'you can leave now.'

'Yes, good,' Tallulah muttered and started walking towards the exit.

Before she could reach the door, McGregor stepped out in front of her.

'What you got there sweetheart? Behind your back,' he bawled, getting the attention of Goldsmith and Wanikiy.

'Nothing,' she stammered taking a step back.

'Show me your hands!' McGregor said, relishing this small moment of power.

Tallulah took another step back whilst all three men watched on.

'What is this?' said Wanikiy 'Show them your hands Tallulah and leave.'

Slowly Tallulah bought her hands out in front of her and held them before McGregor, his smile slowly turning to a scowl as she held out her empty palms.

'Can I leave now?' Tallulah ridiculed. McGregor stood firm.

'Oh, for God sake McGregor, let her out of here. We've more important things to do than search children,' Goldsmith said looking to Wanikiy for approval and shaking his head dismissively.

Tallulah walked out the door without so much as a goodbye to her father and kept walking. Walking past the stores, past the armory, past the dormitories, past the mess hall and into the female shower area which was currently unoccupied. She opened one of the shower cubicles and put her hand on the wall holding back the sickness rising from her stomach. She reached into the waistband of her jeans and pulled out the vial and held it up in front of her eyes.

'So, you are the apocalypse,' she said and began to cry.

CHAPTER EIGHT

Tonight was the night and everyone was nervous. Logan had spent the last two days listening to the plans of the President and his assembly room cohorts and knew exactly what was happening and when. His hope was that after the guards they planned to knock out were replaced, they would realize the group had left the base straight away. However, instead of coming to the assumption that something was occurring with the plan to distribute the toxin, they would be more concerned that the children had left the facility.

At 1.00 am most of the team had assembled in Logan's room and were discussing last minute plans when Faye walked into the room with Zack Stoker, a boy from Danny's dormitory. In all honesty Danny couldn't stand the guy. Zack was blonde haired and looked like he'd been chiseled out of granite. Smug and pretentious he thought he was better than everyone else. Back in the day he would've been an all-star quarterback, but here and now he was just a good looking nobody who wanted to be a somebody.

'What's going on?' Logan said.

'It's Jay,' Faye said on the verge of tears, 'He's slipped and fractured his skull. Zack found him and told me. I panicked. I didn't know what to do. I told Zack everything and he's agreed to help,' said Faye.

Logan didn't like this at all, but at this point he knew options were limited. He needed the manpower and as paranoid as this made him, he knew that now Zack knew their plans there was no leaving him behind.

'What actually happened? Is Jay going to be ok?' said Logan

Zack stepped forward grinning. 'I was walking past his parents living quarters when I heard a noise. I went to investigate and found Jay lying in the middle of the room, guns and ammunition everywhere. Thought he'd done himself in at first. Then realized he must've have slipped or something. There was blood all over the kitchen floor. Of course, the guns got me thinking something was going on so I bagged them up, stashed them, then called the medical team. They said he's critical but stable. No idea when, or if, he might wake up. Bad news for him but good news for you. I get to help you '*save the world*' and you get an all-American hero on your side.'

Faye punched him weakly on the arm and then looked at him in awe forgetting her friend who was lying in the base hospital.

'You were the only one there?' said Logan.

'Yeah man, like I said. I got the guns,' he winked at Logan. There was no going back now.

'Looks like you're in then. Faye, get Zack up to speed. Firstly, though I need to talk you all through Danny's part in the plan. We don't know what's going to happen and I can't take the chance that something happens to me out there, so you all need to be aware of Plan B. If we don't get to the Professor in time or if he can't make an antidote it's down to Danny.' He looked at Danny. 'Danny will take one of the military motorbikes to the reservoir and wait there for our signal. If we fail then either myself, or one of you, will contact Danny through the walkie talkie and he will blow the reservoir foundations. In theory this will cut off water supply to the territories it flows too, and the toxin will have no way of travelling through the water system.' He stopped and picked up something from the table beside him and handed it to Danny. 'This explosive trigger is rigged so that once you press it the explosive is live. Once you remove your finger from the trigger the charges will explode. Now the most important part. There is only one pressure point in the reservoir according to the blueprints which will blow the whole place and it's at the most central point of the dam. Even more importantly you cannot release the trigger within one hundred meters of the explosives, or you'll be caught up in the blast. Do you understand?'

'Let's see,' Danny mused. 'Travel across a country I've not seen in years on a motorbike I don't really know how to ride, plant a bomb in the heart of a water reservoir potentially infested with android technology and make sure I get out of there before it either blows me up or I get drowned? I get the gist Bro.'

'That's about it Danny boy,' said Logan. 'Are we ready guys?'

They nodded quietly.

Logan picked up a gun from the table and handed it barrel first to Zack 'Ever fired a gun?'

The base was quiet with everyone asleep in their rooms or dorms. The only people working through the night were either the lab technicians or the military. There were security cameras, but they hadn't been switched on in years. There was no need. So, getting to the base exit was the easy part. Faye and Danny were the sharpshooters and lined up the tranquilizer guns at the two guards who were in the right place at the right time. So far so good. Logan counted down quietly 'Three, Two, One, fire' and the whistle of the darts went through the air, one of the guards slapping at his neck where the dart hit and then both slumping to the floor.

The exit ramp was hydraulic, and Logan hit the switch to open the ramp leading to the empty town above them. Nothing happened.

'Logan?' Tallulah said. He hit the switch again and the ramp started to move. He breathed a sigh of relief and put a hand on Tallulah's shoulder.

'Guys get yourselves and the guns into the jeep. It's showtime,' said Tallulah.

Danny stopped Logan before he got into the jeep and pulled him to one side. 'I know I've been a stubborn idiot and I know we haven't spoken for way too long, but I need to tell you something.'

'Tell me when we've stopped all this and are back safe and sound,' said Logan.

'Logan. We are doing the right thing aren't we? I mean not telling dad.'

'He's blinded by Goldsmith and the rest of those snakes trying to save themselves. He's a good man Danny, but even good men make mistakes.' He put his head against Danny's. 'Take care little brother. We're counting on you.'

Logan got into the jeep alongside Tallulah and lent over and kissed her on the cheek 'He loves you. You know that right? As in, he's in love with you.'

'I know,' she replied and kissed him back.

The jeep pulled away and headed up the ramp and into the unknown. A few yards out of the tunnel a lone figure on a motorbike flew past the jeep with its shadow raising a hand as it cut across in front of the headlamps and veered off right while the jeep continued straight on.

Only a few hours had past and already the sun was starting to rise. The desert was already getting hot and the back of a stuffy jeep was already taking its toll on the crew who weren't used to being above ground or the constant bumping of a jeep going over almost non-existent roads.

Scott and Seth were the only ones who genuinely looked like they were enjoying themselves whilst even Xander had stopped chain smoking and was looking a shade of green. Brad had been squirming for a good twenty minutes and stuck his head through to the front of the jeep. 'Any chance of a pee break?' He said.

'Give it five minutes,' replied Logan. 'The satellite imaging shows that there's a gas station ten miles up. We're not desperate but if we can replace the gas we've already used it'll be a bonus.' Brad nodded and sat down again, slightly more relieved than he was before.

Ten minutes later they arrived at the Gas station and pulled in close to one of the pumps. The station was abandoned and no-one had been there in a long time. The windows were covered in sand and dirt and the petrol pumps had long rusted and were empty. 'Worth a quick look inside?' said Chuck to Logan. 'Yes. Take the twins and be careful. Guns up always. Take no chances.'

Scott and Seth were already circling around by the door so when Chuck gave them the nod they smiled at one another and opened the door to the shop. It was empty with only a few can's littering the floor and shelves. 'Hey, found a candy bar,' shouted Seth to his sibling. Seth lifted the bar of chocolate and squinted, looking at some string tied around it. In that split second he realized that he'd made a huge mistake and before he could look up to where the string ended an arrow from a spring-loaded crossbow was a meter from his face.

Seth closed his eyes awaiting the inevitable but when it didn't come he opened one eye slowly and then another, his heart pounding in his chest. He blinked and looked at Scott standing next to him holding a baseball bat with an arrow sticking out of it. 'It's a waste of a good bat if you ask me,' said Scott. 'Would've done less damage to that head of yours,' he chuckled.

'Let's get the Hell out of dodge boys. There's nothing but trouble here and we've already got enough of that on the horizon,' said Chuck.

'Find anything?' shouted Logan

'Candy bar?' said Seth, all too happy to give away the thing he'd almost died for.

'Ooh.' Brad's eyes lit up hungrily.

'Really dude? It's been two hours,' Zack said nastily.

'Let's get going. Back in the jeep,' said Logan, hoping to get further ahead and closer to their goal.

By Logan's timings he had hoped to be in Mississippi within the ten hours it would take for anyone to realize they had gone missing. They then had to make their way to the prison and get into the prison without raising suspicion before tracking down the Professor. Truthfully, he had hoped that when everyone back at the base had realized they had gone missing that his father would stop the plan to release the toxin. Instead choosing to send a search party out for them. But he knew his father and he knew that it wouldn't take him and the other board members long to realize exactly what they were up to and push the plan into action immediately.

Danny had further to go to the reservoir in Nebraska but with a good head start and with avoiding any major towns or cities Logan hoped he would have an easier journey. The reservoir was far enough from civilization that human beings would hopefully not be around to slow his brother down. The robotic system to keep the water flowing to the other states was a static system, unlike some of the android systems which were used at the nuclear plants. But Nebraska was where his father's military would be heading as soon as they had cottoned on to what was happening and he feared they would not let Danny stand in the way.

****

Across the country Danny had made good progress, even with adjusting for the brightness of natural light and breathing in fresh air for the first time in forever. He stopped the motorbike in between two hills and looked down onto the valley below him. Everything was brown and dusty, not the green he remembered as a child. No plants lived here anymore and neither did any wildlife. If it had, it would have been hunted for food long ago. The skull of some kind of deer lay nearby and he got off the motorbike and picked it up trying to tap into the dead animals soul 'Let's not end up like you my friend,' he said to himself and put the skull on the front of the bike, took a swig of water from his canteen, glimpsed at his map and then set off again.

Not much further on and the road was beginning to blur in front of him and he lifted the visor on his helmet to rub his eyes. No doubt about it his eyesight was progressively getting worse and he pulled to a stop on the deserted highway. Looking around he couldn't see anything except the horizon in every direction. He stumbled from the bike and sat down cross legged on the floor dizzy. His head felt heavy and his eyes rolled back into his head as he slumped backwards against the motorbike.

****

Tallulah tried Danny on the walkie talkie again 'Tallulah to Danny, do you read? Over.' She hung her head, waited twenty seconds and repeated the message. Nothing. 'This isn't good Logan,' she looked up biting her lip. 'What if he's had an accident? What if the walkie talkie is broken and we can't let him know if we fail?'

'What if he's riding between two canyons? What if he's so focused on getting to the reservoir that the walkie talkie is in his backpack? What if, what if? We can't afford to think like that Tals. These are satellite communications so they will work anywhere in the world. He's probably just not heard it and once he stops he will contact us.'

She looked unconvinced but went back to plotting the route on the navigation system.

'What you said back at the base, about Danny,' she said without looking up.

'He's always loved you. I knew back then, and I knew he wouldn't do anything about it, but I knew I had to. Does that make me a bad person?'

'No, of course not. It means you took a chance and it paid off. He was my best friend, but it was always you Logan. Danny was a danger to himself and everyone around him, but you made me feel safe and wanted. You made me love you and you were the one who was there for me when I needed someone to look after me when my father didn't. It was meant to be,' she said reassuring him.

'I will always be there for you Tals, always' Logan said looking at her then back towards the road.

From nowhere a loud bang sounded on the roof of the jeep just above Logan's head 'Dude, you know we can hear you back here?' Faye shouted through the window. Tallulah and Logan smiled at each other and she put her hand on his knee.

The jeep juddered sharply 'What?' Logan looked at the petrol gage. 'Something isn't right.' The jeep coughed and spluttered to a halt.

'What's going on?' said Chuck jumping out the back of the jeep followed by the others.

'It's the gas. The gage says we're out, but back at the gas station we had three quarters of a tank. Plenty to get us to the prison.' Logan walked round to the petrol tank. 'Shhhhh, argh. It's leaking. We've lost a whole tank of fuel thanks to a goddamn hole.' He grimaced and put his hand on his head, walking around trying to think. 'Right, we patch up the tank, use the spare tanks of fuel and hope we come across some kind of vehicle in the next thirty miles or so.'

'Logan, I hate to break this to you man, but what spare tanks,' said Chuck, 'there aren't any.'

'What? These jeeps all have two spare tanks as standard,' he said running around the side of the jeep refusing to believe what he'd been told. 'No, No, No.'

'Calm down,' Tallulah put both her hands on his shoulders.

'Calm down? This puts us five hours outside where we need to be without transport.'

'So, we walk until we find some other way of getting there. We don't give up,' she replied.

Xander who had walked a good twenty feet from the group to light up a cigarette shouted over 'She's right you know. We didn't come this far to give up now,' and flicked his match onto the floor igniting a trail of petrol behind the jeep. 'Oh Shhhh.'

The group scattered throwing themselves to the floor watching the jeep explode in front of their eyes.

Once the flames had died down, they came back together, and Logan gathered them around looking each of them down in turn. 'Xander was right,' he said.

'You mean before he blew up our only means of transport and limited supplies?' Chuck smiled.

'We have come too far to give up. People's lives depend on us. We've lived a glorified life compared to the people in these cities and now our families want them dead so we can thrive. This is our time and that should be our decision, not theirs. I say we fight. For the people to make their own choices and for us to make our own choice. There's no going back now.'

The group picked up what food and water they could salvage along with their weapons and started the long walk in the middle of the highway.

'Wait, what's that in the distance?' said Brad, his eyes widening. 'It's a person. It's an actual person.'

CHAPTER NINE

As they got closer, they could see that it was a person walking closer towards them. Still some hundred yards away they could make out that it was a man, or what was once a man but now a skeleton wearing skin. The sagging empty flesh hung from his half naked body; his modesty only covered by some oversized briefs like a diaper. The man's head was lowered, and he hadn't lifted it since Brad had alerted them that he was there.

The closer they got to him the more they noticed how he resembled a corpse rather than a living, breathing, person. His arms swung either side of his body as if they no longer had any use and his legs on the verge of breaking, but somehow, he moved forward getting ever closer to the group. Logan lifted his hand and made a fist indicating the others to stop, though Brad was still out in front, smiling at the fact that this was the first contact they had had with the outside world since leaving the base.

'Brad. Step back. Let me handle this,' Logan shouted out.

Brad just stopped in his tracks, mouth gaping at the man who appeared not to even notice them. Logan raised his gun towards the man suspicious of who he was and where he had come from. They were still some way from the city limits, and they hadn't heard any vehicles approaching. There was wilderness in pretty much every direction. It was like the man had appeared out of thin air.

'Hey you. Stop,' he shouted. But again, the man kept walking and was now within ten yards of Brad. 'Stop.' Finally, the man cocked his head slightly, acknowledging Logan, but still staring at the ground in front of him and came to a standstill.

'Sir, hello. My name is Logan Mathers. Who are you? What is your name?' he spoke slowly, concisely and loud enough that the man would hear. 'We are heading into the city. Do you know how much further it is? Would you like some water?'

The man stood completely still as if he was a statue. No sign that he had heard what Logan had said and no indication as to what his next move might be. Zack chuckled 'freaking Zombie.'

Logan looked back at him and scowled taking a few steps forward towards Brad and the man. 'Look, we have water, we can help you. What is your name?'

The eerie silence of no-one speaking made the fact the man wasn't moving extremely unnerving for everyone except Brad, who was a buzz of nervous excitement.

'I'm Brad,' he chirped. 'From Texas,' he held out his hand and shuffled forward. 'We're here to help you. Well everyone really.'

'Brad,' Chuck worriedly spoke up. His voice more croaky than normal.

The man looked to try and raise his head, which looked like too much effort on his part. But Brad heard something. A whisper.

'Guys, he spoke. Hey, don't be scared man. What did you say?'

The man's lips were now visible, although his face was not. His wispy hair was blowing in the very slight desert air and a noise, almost a very quiet whistle came from his mouth.

'What?' Brad said again, edging ever closer to the man. Logan followed, moving closer to Brad but keeping his distance and position away from the stranger. Again, the man tried to talk but the dryness of his throat just made a noise. 'What?' Brad was in touching distance now and along with the man everyone else was frozen, all with their guns aimed directly at him.

'Food,' the man said.

Brad's eyes lit up. 'He just wants food,' he said smiling and turning around to the others.

In a split second the man reached for Brad and raised his head to reveal two dark sunken pits where his eyes should have been. The glimmer of the sun caught on the man's mouth full of sharp razor teeth like a shark and his head jolted to the side. 'My, you're a fleshy one aren't you,' he growled, and the teeth cut into Brad neck ripping skin away from his throat, blood spurting everywhere.

Logan's heart was racing, and he fell backwards onto the ground, away from Brad and the man, horror on his face and for only the second time in his life he was scared. So, this was one of the monsters that he had heard about in rumors around the base from the other soldiers. He had laughed it off like a firepit ghost story. Brad's face was contorted, still smiling and looking at the others as if nothing had happened, meanwhile he had fallen to his knees and the man had straddled him and was eating into him as if he was prime rib.

Faye was the first one to fire, spraying bullets towards the man which she half expected to bounce off this sub-human being feasting on their friend. This shocked the others into action and soon bullets were coming from everywhere cutting the predator almost in half. Logan was horizontal on the floor but had regained his composure, lined up his shot and pulled the trigger on his handgun watching his bullet in slow motion as it cracked through the man's forehead.

The sound of shells hitting the ground stopped, and again there was silence, apart from a spluttering gurgling sound which was coming from Brad. Logan stood up, looked around at the others and moved forward to Brad and the man who was now just parts of a body scattered on the earth. Xander retched and then puked, then lit up a cigarette.

'What the Hell was that?' said Seth, which gave permission for everyone to start talking at once, looking at each other for reassurance that this wasn't a nightmare and that they were in fact awake and looking at the body of their dead friend.

'Is this what we're fighting for?' Zack held his hands up. 'For monsters?'

Logan looked taken aback as if in that moment everything he thought they were doing had been a mistake and in those few seconds of pausing the others saw it too.

'We don't know that they are all like this,' Tallulah came to his rescue. 'In fact, the intelligence that we have back at the base would all but confirm otherwise. We've heard the stories sure, and there is no smoke without fire, but for all we know he could have been living out here in the wilderness by himself for days, maybe weeks or months. Imagine what that does to a person's mind, without food or water.' She looked down at Brad. 'If we give up now then he died for nothing. If we go on and we all die then at least we died, like Brad, trying to do something good in this world. I'm going on and you can either follow me and finish what we started, or you can turn back and admit that you will never ever be in control of your life.'

'I'm with you girl,' Chuck bawled at Tallulah.

'Thank you,' Logan mouthed towards Tallulah. 'Let's bury our friend.'

****

When Danny awoke, he was disorientated, and the night was drawing in around him. He pulled himself up against the motorcycle and squinting tried to put together the pieces of what happened before he passed out. His mouth was dry and sandy but as he went to put his water bottle to his mouth he instinctively stopped and instead of drinking he put the canteen to his nose and sniffed the liquid. The last thing he remembered was taking a swig of water and not long after passing out. The water didn't smell out of the ordinary, but that wasn't to say there was nothing wrong with it. Instead he took a half full bottle of Coca-Cola out of his jacket pocket on his bike and swilled the warm coke around in his mouth, spitting it out and then necking back the remainder of the bottle. His paranoia was kicking in and as he could think of no good reason why he would have passed out he had every right to be paranoid.

Danny looked at his watch to see how far behind schedule he was and clacked his tongue against the roof of his mouth in disapproval. 'Never mind,' he said out loud to himself. His part of the plan meant he had a bit of time on his side, but he needed to be in place when the call came, so he jumped to his feet and back onto his motorbike. The walkie talkie was tucked in the front of the bike and he pulled it out of its holder and turned it on.

'Logan. Come in Logan, over.' The radio crackled static.

'Logan. Come in Logan, over.' Nothing.

He wiped the sweat from his forehead and listened to the walkie talkie. Other than the crackling he could hear a buzzing, but it didn't seem to be coming from the radio. *A bird perhaps*? He switched the walkie talkie back off and looked around. It was feint but he heard something in the distance that spooked him. He switched the walkie talkie back on.

'Logan. Come in Logan, over.' Silence.

He slumped over the handlebars dejected, when the radio feedback almost made him fall backwards off the bike. 'This is Logan. Danny, are you there? Over.'

'Thank God Logan. I thought this goddamn radio was busted. Are you ok? Over.'

'We're a bit busted up ourselves brother, but we're still here, over.'

'Are you at the city yet? Over.'

'Not yet. We've had some transport issues. In that it blew up, over.'

'Jeez! Is everyone ok, over?'

'Brad didn't make it man. Long story, but he's dead. You ok?' Logan let it hang in the air to give Danny a moment to take in what he just said 'over.' The radio went quiet.

'You give him a good send off?' Danny replied 'over.'

'Best we could. You not at the reservoir yet, over?'

'Had a few issues of my own but getting back on track. Heading back on the road now, over.'

Danny heard the sound again, buzzing behind him, like the sound of another motorcycle but a good thirty miles away but carrying in the emptiness of the vast wasteland.

'We're going to get a couple of hours rest and then get back on it. Hope to be in the city by tomorrow at eleven hundred hours and head for the prison, over.'

'Got a plan to get in there yet? Over,' said Danny.

'Swing and a prayer Brother, over.' Danny felt Logan's smile through the airwaves.

'Look man, I got to get on the road. I've got a bad feeling that I'm not going to be alone for too much longer. I'll be in touch tomorrow before you hit the city, over.'

'Take care Danny. Be careful. Some of those horror stories you heard aren't just stories, over.'

'They never are buddy, they never are, over and out.'

Danny put the walkie talkie back into its holder, switched his headlight on and turned the key on the bike. He took one last look behind him and put his foot down on the gas.

****

Back on the base the war room was full of governors and board members stood around talking frantically trying to get an update on what had happened. They had been called there because of an incident which involved two of the soldiers guarding the base being drugged. That was the limit of their knowledge and, as yet, they were unaware that the group led by Logan were missing.

The President pushed through the door flanked by Goldsmith and followed by Wanikiy. He looked flustered and stood behind his chair at the head of table, his brow furrowed, and his bottom lip pinched between his finger and thumb. He lifted his hand and without saying anything he signaled for everyone to sit. Goldsmith took his seat around the table whilst a soldier brought a chair for Wanikiy. The President coughed and took a long drink from the water in front of him. 'We have some bad news I am afraid. During the night and early morning, a number of young adults on the base used tranquilizers to get passed our exit guards and have left the base.' Everyone around the room looked at each other in shock. 'Both my sons are amongst those who have left.'

'Mr President,' Pitkin stuttered. 'Do we know why they have escaped the base?'

'Escaped?' Goldsmith interrupted 'a strange choice of words.' Pitkin visibly withdrew into himself.

'At this time, we do not know why they left the base, but I can assure you that we are doing everything within our power using our surveillance and satellite imaging to find out where they are and if they are safe. I have already spoken with the parents of the other children missing and as you can see there are some noticeable absences from the room.' Until now no-one had noticed the empty seats at the table but now each one of them was working out whose children had gone AWOL. 'For now, I would ask that you give myself and the rest of the military search team some space to work out what has happened and how we can get them back. Please give them your utmost support. I will be addressing the rest of the base shortly and providing updates when I can. Please, for now, go back to your living areas until further notice.'

The room stood and started to disperse, each one of them still in shock and whispering to the closest person to them for any kind of information that might shed more light on what the president had just told them.

When the last person had left the room and just The President, Goldsmith and Wanikiy remained. Goldsmith closed the door firmly behind them and stood silently with his back to the other two men.

'Now, tell me, what the Hell is going on?' The President spitted through his teeth to Goldsmith.

Goldsmith turned with both palms down in a motion for The President to calm down, which was not going to happened until he started to get answers.

'Truthfully,' he said, 'We don't know.'

'Are you seriously telling me that nine children, left the comfort of a base with food and drink to experience living in a world of famine and violence. Let's get this straight, we are not talking about any children either. These kids are clever, my boys included, not to mention your Tallulah. Did she say anything?'

Wanikiy shook his head and Goldsmith held up his hand before the scientist could speak.

'Look, at this moment in time we know as much as you do Sir and are working on getting them back as soon as we can. We can't assume to know what is going on in a teenager's head or why they have chosen to leave the base. I've got my best men on it. Trust me, I care about those kids as much as anyone on this base,' Goldsmith feigned genuine sincerity.

The President raised his eyebrows at this comment. 'Make sure you have. I want regular updates every hour and I want a search party out as soon as you have pinpointed their whereabouts.' With that he stormed past Goldsmith and out of the room.

Goldsmith made a noise of distain once the door closed and then beckoned through the window for the two soldiers standing outside the room to come in.

'Are our men in place and do they have eyes on the target?' Goldsmith snorted.

'Sir yes sir. I believe Soldier M has eyes on target two and should make contact within a day, if required,' said one of the soldiers.

Goldsmith thought about this. 'No. No contact until I say so. How's the kid in the infirmary?'

'Still out Sir,' the soldier barked.

Goldsmith nodded towards the door and both soldiers marched out.

'So, still think everyone is onboard?' Wanikiy spoke up.

'We knew someone would oppose it. We just didn't know it'd be the

President's own son. Oh, and did I mention your daughter?'

'Maybe if you didn't have me working 18-hour days in that laboratory I could have convinced her it was the only option available to us,' said Wanikiy.

'It's fine, we have it covered. We know where Logan's little group is and how close the younger Mathers is to Operation Nebraska. Everything is under control. McGregor has his end covered and this little prison scenario is a non-starter. For all we know your ex-partner Brittle was killed a long time ago in that place, as per the original plan,' he tutted. 'As soon as we knew their plan, we put the safety net in place. The operation to release the toxin into the water supply goes ahead as planned and nothing will get in our way.'

'And the safety of those kids out there?'

Goldsmith gritted his teeth 'The second they decided to go against the board of the United States Government,' he said waving his hand around the room at the empty seats 'they put themselves at risk. That wasn't a decision we made, but it's one we now have to deal with.'

Wanikiy looked now his glasses at Goldsmith 'Have you even once consider that these kids know what they are doing and maybe, just maybe they could succeed.'

'You're delusional man. Brittle couldn't have survived in there. Besides, as I told you, we have precautions in place to take care of anything unexpected,' a smirk stretched across his face.

'Like the boy in the infirmary?' Wanikiy countered.

'Collateral damage. McGregor can sometimes go overboard but he gets the job done.'

'And keeping the president in the dark?'

'All these questions Wanikiy? It sounds like you want this mission to fail. Do you have some kind of death wish? I told you. The less he knows the better. The second he knows that them leaving had something to do with the toxin he will put a hold on the operation, and we are effectively killing ourselves. Let's get it done and worry about getting them back after we know we have somewhere for them to come back to.'

'Don't forget that my daughter is out there Goldsmith. I have more to lose than anyone.'

'And don't forget you and your daughter are only alive because I allowed it. It could easily have been you rotting in that prison too remember.'

Wanikiy gave him a sideways glance and pushed his glasses up the bridge of his nose in disgust.

'I hope you know what you are doing?'

'What we are doing Wanikiy. What we are doing.'

CHAPTER TEN

Danny's eyes were starting to blur in the dark and it felt like he had been riding for days, not hours. He needed to rest and pulled over to the side of the highway as a precaution, momentarily forgetting the complete lack of traffic. He had passed the odd car abandoned in the middle of the road, swerving last minute on several occasions as the parked cars came out of the pitch black. Out here everything was stationery. He took a bite from a chocolate bar which was now melted goo, but it gave him a much-needed boost. Whatever had made him pass out had seriously slowed down his ability to think on his feet and in honesty he was still a little groggy. Still he heard the buzzing from before, albeit it slightly louder now. He knew for sure now what he had thought before. It was another motorbike.

He didn't panic, but he was aware that he needed to do something to stop whoever was following him. Thoughts ran through his head. Maybe it was a scout sent ahead of the convoy with the toxin or maybe it was someone who had been living above ground who saw him and was trying to catch up with him. Could it be someone who could help him? He doubted this very much and again his paranoia led him back to the conclusion that not only did his father and the others now know they had left the base, but that they were aware of the plan to thwart the toxin getting to the reservoir. His heart skipped as he wondered if the others had already been caught. Would they be taken back to base and be disciplined, or would it be more serious. He knew that if Goldsmith had anything to do with it they'd be locked up in the base jails. Surely his father wouldn't allow that. Danny felt they had a genuine grievance against the plan to annihilate half the remaining country.

Previously the buzzing had been distant and looking into the dark Danny was positive he could see a spot of light on the horizon. It was hard to tell how far ahead he was, but he knew he still had an edge on his newfound friend. However, once he reached his destination, he would have to face whoever was following him head on. Something he didn't relish, especially as his part in the plan involved being in a certain place at a very specific time. If he wasn't there and the others failed, then they failed altogether.

Danny took some wire from his backpack and started to stretch it across the road at waist height, securing one end to part of a dried-out tree stump and the other to a pile of rocks. It wouldn't kill his pursuer, but it would seriously slow them down and potentially put their bike out of action. Once he'd set up his booby trap, he waited ten more minutes and then took off on his bike. Feeling refreshed he rode for another ten miles and then rolled the motor bike around to look behind him. He could hear the buzzing, louder still and the spot of light was becoming more of a beam. The other bike must have been close to the wire by now and Danny waited and waited and waited, but nothing.

Had the wire fallen loose or had the person behind him seen it in time and driven around the trap. Danny started to panic and considered hiding out until the person had passed. It would mean giving away his advantage of getting to the reservoir first and finding a prime place to see the person approaching. His heart was thumping against his chest and he started to feel sick.

Then the buzzing stopped, and the beam started moving from side to side. A louder noise like something mechanic grinding filled the air in the distance, and then nothing. It had worked. Danny let his head drop and breathed a sigh of relief. As he did, he heard a 'whoomph' noise and saw flames shooting thirty feet in the air. 'Please God don't let that be anyone on our side,' he said to himself. For a split second he considered driving back to see what had happened but thought better of it.

****

McGregor had been following Danny for some time after Goldsmith had got wind of Logan's plan for him to travel to the reservoir. He knew that, had Goldsmith known about the contingency plan for Danny to go to the reservoir earlier, he would have caught up to Danny hours ago, and as per Goldsmith's instruction the problem would have been buried six-foot underground already. Still, McGregor enjoyed the chase and as much as he disliked the idea of leaving his nice comfortable home on the base, he knew that it was necessary to continue the life he had become accustomed to. He knew that a day or two on the road and killing a child was a small price to pay for another twenty to thirty years on the planet.

McGregor knew that Danny would have to drink from his water bottle at some point, which had been drugged by Goldsmith's mole before Danny had left the base. *'Bloody kids think the world owes them. Live in the real world first and then see how you feel,'* he thought to himself as he sped down the highway. It was getting darker and without a helmet his eyes were starting to tear up with the cold cross wind. He didn't know how far ahead Danny was, but he knew that he was in touching distance, and he rode through blurred vision, putting his foot down harder.

It happened so fast McGregor didn't have time to think or act. The wire across the road cut into the front tire and wrapped itself around the wheel. As the wheel buckled the bike crashed sideways and the wire wrapped around the handlebars. McGregor's wrist was trapped as the bike slid to a stop pinning him to the floor.

McGregor's face throbbed where a layer of skin had been removed by the road. He couldn't feel his legs. He tugged at the wire wrapped around his arm. Thinking as quickly as he could, he reached for his knife and tried to cut at the wire, unsuccessfully. He looked at his wrist then back to the knife and quickly put out of his mind what he was thinking. 'I'd rather die,' he mumbled. He started to unravel the wire when he smelt gasoline leaking from the back of the bike. Jerking loose the wire he dragged himself from under the bike and up onto his feet. His legs felt numb, but he was ok. The bike caught alight and he stepped away from the fast-rising flames, now burning where he was laying not ten seconds ago. The flame caught the gasoline and went up to the sky and then it was gone, back down to nothing more than the flame from a match. McGregor shrugged. 'Could this day get any worse?'

McGregor turned back to the road to continue his journey by foot, but when he looked around he had been surrounded by three shabby wolves slowly starting to edge in. 'Really? I mean really. You let me walk away from that and now this.' McGregor reached for his knife.

****

Danny was close to the reservoir and he could hear water travelling ahead of him. Now it was a case of getting inside, setting up the explosives and sitting firm until he either heard from Logan, or he didn't. The sun was starting to come up and the dam become visible in the distance.

The past two days had felt strange with no-one other than himself for company and only the hum of his own motorbike filled the air. The odd bird flew high in the sky away from predators but for the most part only the world moved alongside him as he rode through wastelands and smallholdings. Passing empty towns only made him more aware of the situation and filled him with trepidation of what was really going on in the world. But the thought of meeting another human being in this apocalyptic nightmare scared him more and more as he realized the severity of being out here alone, with no-one else and with no food.

He passed a small group of houses, which had probably been occupied by workers at the reservoir. Danny imagined the workers coming home to their families after a hard day's work and sitting down with them, talking about their day. Maybe the fathers played baseball with their sons or daughters in the yard. Perhaps they would meet up with their neighbors for games night, or drinks and BBQ on balmy evenings in summertime.

He slowed down and pulled up outside one of the houses which faced directly onto the highway. Not many cars came through here, even when these houses thrived. It was a one-way road to the reservoir. He stepped up onto the porch and open the door, half hanging off its hinges. He felt like he was intruding and considered shouting out, but then caught himself and stopped before the noise left his mouth. The door opened to a dining room filled with a table and chairs around it. Only one plate was laid out with a knife and fork either side.

Danny checked the cupboards even though he had ample supplies, just as a back-up. As expected, they were empty. The floorboards creaked with each step he took, and he felt the wood disintegrating as he started up the stairs. He didn't even know why he had stopped at the house, but he was drawn to it. He looked in the bedrooms one by one.

The first room was pink and that of a young girl, maybe seven or eight, dolls neatly lined up on the top of her bookcase and tucked in her bed. He watched the girl running through the room shouting '*daddy, daddy*' whilst laughing and her dress flowing behind her. Then into the boy's room, bunkbeds and a small cot-bed. A snotty nosed toddler stood on the cot watching whilst his brothers played with penknives and play tic tac toe. This house had always been devoid of computers, mobile phones and the anti-social technology the major cities thrived on.

Finally, into the last bedroom where the husband held his wife's face in his hands and smiling kissed her on the lips, happy that his little family were together, and that life was good. He provided for them and they gave him love in return. Back downstairs they sat down at the table with the boys filling their plates and everyone speaking at the same time. The youngest child with food around his mouth grinning at his mother, whilst father cut the meat and passed around the plate. Danny sat down at the table with the family, breathing in the memory, but then they were gone, dust in the air as if they had never even existed.

Danny stood up and walked back out onto the porch, glancing up to the bedroom where the small skeletons lay together in the double bed, hands still entwined. He sat down on the porch swing next to the remains of the father, jawbone missing and skull in pieces, shotgun laid out in front of him.

****

As the sun started to come up McGregor pulled the wolfskin over his shoulders and rubbed his hands in front of a fire. A home-made spit above the fire held the remains of one of the wolves and he reached out and wrenched off a body part and crunched into the meat and bone. 'Looks like I made a 'dogs' dinner' of you Fido,' he laughed.

CHAPTER ELEVEN

Logan soon realized that the group were getting tired and need a break. They had been walking for hours and although they knew they were getting close to the city morale was low and they were all hungry and thirsty and in need of a rest. In the distance they could make out high rise buildings and knew that they had maybe two or three more hours before they would be at their first destination. What they didn't know was what to expect from the city itself. If the creature that attacked Brad was anything to go by, they were heading for a warzone and every one of them knew it. Unfortunately, the only way to Parchman Prison was right through the city center.

Logan stopped and drank from his water bottle. The others saw this as an opportunity and did the same. Chuck sat down with his arms stretched out. The twins did the same and Seth pulled off his boots and emptied the sand from them. No-one spoke but they were all thinking about Brad, and that anyone of them could be next. Xander lit up a cigarette.

'We'll go on another hour and then make camp for a few hours. Then we head into the city and make our way to the prison. I get it that you're tired and demoralized, but we're so close now. You're scared, and I understand that too, but it took guts to get this far. I'm not going to promise you that we're all going to make it, but I promise you that I will do everything I can to make sure that we do. Everything is within our grasp to ensure we make the right decision to save these people.' As the words were coming out his mouth, Logan was wondering whether he believed it himself. He had to. He started this journey and had got all these kids involved in something far bigger than just his moral compass. He'd already lost one of his team and he wasn't about to lose anyone else.

Seth sighed and pulled his boots back on. They started off again, one foot in front of each other. No further than ten minutes up the road Logan stopped again. 'Did you hear that?' he whispered to Tallulah. She shook her head. 'There, I heard it again.'

The rest of the group had stopped and were all looking around in the dark with their flashlights, trying to see what Logan was hearing. 'I don't hear anything dude,' said Chuck.

Logan stared in the black abyss of the desert, squinting towards where he thought the sound was coming from. He moved forward slowly and raised his torched. Two small lights shined back at him. He moved forward again towards the lights, which looked to be moving around. Five yards from the lights he switched his torch to full beam to see a gaunt brown bear hunched over the half-eaten body of a man. The bear looked up at Logan and locked eyes with him. Logan slowly retreated, and the bear went back to its meal while the beam of light faded, and both the bear and the body became invisible into the night again.

The others were huddled together shaking. Tallulah had her hand over her mouth to stop herself screaming, and Faye was holding her still. Logan raised his hand and pointed forward and they moved slowly away and towards the city.

A few hours later the sun was starting to come up and they were entering the city. Eerily quiet the empty roads made no sound. No traffic, no people and no shops made this a spooky place to be. They had seen what happened to human beings living in this world and they didn't want to meet anymore. Sometimes it's the not knowing what's out there that scares us, more than the reality. In this case it was both.

Logan looked at the map and then looked in three different directions 'This way,' he said and moved confidently forward. By his reckoning they weren't far, as the prison was pretty much on the outskirts of town. Something to do with it being home to some of the country's worst criminal offenders. The intel he had from military records showed that through the city's police station there were tunnels leading to the main gantry in the prison. Not even the previous guards had known about these as they hadn't been used in years. The government had full access to blueprints though and Logan had planned to get access through the Police Station and into the prison that way.

His expectations at this point were that everyone in that prison was dead already, including the Professor, but somewhere deep inside him he had to believe that everything was still possible. If the others realized that he was losing faith, then it was all over. He had no plan as to what would happen once they were inside the prison, but hoped they were in a better physical condition to fight than anyone they might come up against. At least they had weapons and if it came down to a fire fight, he was confident they could at least get out of there alive.

As they walked down the center of the road, they all had that feeling of being watched from the doorways and windows. The breeze in the air started making garbage move and the group started getting jittery. Tallulah started seeing people at the windows of the shops and on double take they were gone. She took Logan's hand and gripped it hard.

At the end of the road a man in a long brown coat casually walked around the corner. He was followed by a group of five others. Then another group came from the side road and stood waiting for Logan and the others to reach them. They slowly scattered across the road blocking any passage through. Logan's hand fell from Tallulah's and closer to his handgun.

'Hello,' he shouted to the first man. 'We're looking for the police station. Can you tell us if we're close?'

The men looked at each other. They were nauseatingly thin, but somehow almost healthy looking compared to the thing that had killed Brad. They were clean and relatively well-presented bearing in mind the circumstances.

'Isn't no Police Station around here son. Not no more,' the man said.

'We need to get to the Police Station to get some important documents,' said Logan, unsure what to say to the man.

'You look like you're hungry son. Why don't you come join us for dinner?' said the man smiling.

'We've just eaten thank you,' said Xander, clearly from the back of the group.

'Look, that's very kind of you, but we're just passing through. We just need to get to the Police Station and then we're gone again. Can you point us in the right direction?' said Logan.

They heard footsteps and another group of men had come up behind them pushing them further forward. 'I insist,' said the man.

Logan drew his gun from its holster, but he felt the click of a gun against the back of his neck and he holstered it again 'No need for that now son. We'd just like to get to know you all. Find out what a lovely bunch of kids like you are doing in our city.' The man behind Logan took the gun back out of its holster. 'Follow me,' he said.

They followed the group of men to the entrance of building and one of the men pulled up the shutters.

It opened to reveal a large warehouse which was housing many families under tents, tarpaulins and homemade housing. Families who had left their own homes looking for food, unable to return due to the dangers of being separated. They had built a community where they were working together to feed themselves. Food was obviously in short supply but as they walked through the building the smell of cooking was obvious.

'What's your name?' Logan asked the leader.

'They call me Samson,' said the man 'On account of my hair,' he added and shook his long mane. He was a giant of a man and not someone you would mess with. 'As you can tell, we are not use to seeing strangers around here.' The families, particularly the children stared at the group, with some of the younger ones coming up and cupping their hands out in front of them. 'They see people like you, looking the way you are, and it gives them hope. You understand? Dressed well. Fed well. But I'm guessing there's more to it than you just found a decent place with supplies. Am I right? Let me guess. Government?'

'Yes, kind of,' Logan said, not wanting to give anything away, but also wanting to gain his trust.

Tallulah knelt by a girl who had held out her hand. 'I've got a candy bar,' she invited, and the little girl nodded gleefully. Then was joined by five more children. 'I'm sorry, I only had one,' and the children dispersed into the crowds of people.

'Where do you get your food from?' she asked Samson.

'Wherever we can. We scavenge, we hunt animals, we also have an outlet that helps us. The one rule we have is that we do not hurt human beings and we do not turn anyone away who wishes to be part of the community. Everyone has something to offer. You may have seen what we call Savages out there. Men and women who have forgotten what it is to be human. Creatures who have lost their minds to the madness of hunger. That's not us. We are a community and a family. So, you'll understand that when a group of well-fed teenagers, with guns, turn up in our neighborhood that we could be concerned,' said Samson.

'We're not here to hurt anyone. We're here to help,' said Tallulah.

'She's right,' said Logan. 'We are here to save lives.'

Logan went on to tell Samson about the plan the government had put into place to poison the water supply and to roll out the system to supply any survivors with self-sustaining crops and breed animals.

Samson stopped him mid flow and raised his eyebrows at Logan 'So on top of everything we have had thrown at us and endured, now we have to be concerned about our own government killing us off, so that the mighty among us can flourish? Can't say it surprises me son,' he chuckled. 'But water is our main commodity here. It's keeping us alive and sustaining what supplies us and our benefactors have. We cannot let this plan happen. Come into my office.'

They had reached the end of the building and an office which was Samson's home and planning room. Building schematics lined the walls and notes on where they could find food and build their own supplies. While they were not feasting every night, they were alive, and they seemed happy. The children ran around laughing whilst the parents worked or spent time improving their makeshift homes. If the plan had been to merely survive then these people had succeeded.

'Please sit,' Samson beckoned to all of them. He was joined by some of the men Logan recognized from outside. 'These men are my trusted advisers and are at your disposal,' he said.

'You mean you aren't going to kill us,' said Seth, breathing a sigh of relief.

The others looked at him shaking their heads, although slightly relieved themselves that this hadn't panned out like they were expecting.

'We're very grateful Samson, but it's not men that we need. It's one man. A Professor,' said Logan.

Samson looked around at his men 'A Professor you say? Can't say I've seen one around here.'

Logan got the impression that Samson wasn't letting on everything he knew but continued. 'Yes, this Professor can, we hope, create an antidote to the toxin they plan to use in the water. We think he is being kept prisoner in the prison and we really need to get to him, if he's alive.'

'A lot of ifs and buts if you ask me son. How you planning to get into the prison?' he replied.

'We have military schematics to get into the courtyard beyond the main fences through the Police Station which has tunnels running back and forth. We just need safe travel to the Police station, and we can take it from there.'

'Sounds like a big job for a bunch of kids,' said Samson leaning back in his chair with his fingers together and pursed his lips.

Zack tutted 'We got this far, didn't we?' he gloated.

'Be careful young man or this maybe as far as you get,' said a man behind him with tattoos covering much of his face.

'Whatever man, you don't hurt human beings, remember,' said Zack. Logan gently but firmly put a hand on his arm, effectively telling him to shut the Hell up.

'Well remembered,' said Samson 'Although I should point out we reserve the right to let you live as long as it doesn't affect our way of living, otherwise,' he ran his finger across his throat.

'Look,' said Logan 'We're not here for trouble. We are here to help and any help you can give us we are grateful for. Even just directions to the Police Station and then we'll leave.'

'No, No. You're our guests. We will get you were you want to be, but tonight you'll stay here and eat with us. See what we're all about. We will show you survivor hospitality,' said Samson.

Logan nodded and looked at the others 'We should really be leaving.'

'I insist,' said Samson menacingly.

The evening had a celebratory feel about it and Logan wondered if every evening was the same or whether this was for their benefit. They certainly felt like guests of honor, sat at the head table in the makeshift dinner hall, alongside Samson and some of '*the elders*'. Logan sat smiling, watching Tallulah and Faye entertaining the children by dancing around by the light of gasoline lamps. The twins sat chatting to other families and every now and then Seth would laugh one of those belly laughs that set everyone else off laughing too. Zack and Xander sat back, playing it cool, people watching but not getting involved in the shenanigans.

The one thing Logan did know was that this wasn't a community that was struggling. Yes, they had lost loved ones and carried pain, but they put it aside so that the community could thrive and enjoy what life they had left. They were grateful for what they had, and they certainly did not deserve to have got this far to then be poisoned for '*the greater good*'. At every step of this journey Logan had felt reassured that they had made the right decision to try and foil the government and his father's plans. These people had a right to the life that they had built, and he would not let it be taken away.

Samson was loved by these people, but Logan still had something nagging in his head that he wasn't being told the truth. He felt Samson knew something more about the prison that he was letting on, but he wasn't in the mood for confrontation. Tomorrow they would leave for the prison and they would either find the Professor and hope he had the answers, or they would have to rely on Danny to take on his part of the plan. Either way tonight was not the night to start trouble.

Suddenly though, there was a banging on the large warehouse door, and everyone stopped. The music that had been playing was switched off and other than some murmurs from the children everyone fell silent. Samson waved his arm and the men started moving into one of the tents, returning with weapons. Logan wanted to ask what was happening, but in the silence he felt he better not speak up and instead his hand touched the gun in its holster. Chuck came alongside him holding a machete, aware that whoever was outside that gate was not welcome.

Chapter Twelve

The silence seemed to last forever and then banging again on the doorway. Samson's men moved behind the door in a well-rehearsed battle formation, whilst the rest of the families backed away to the far end of the warehouse.

'About fifteen,' one of the men mouthed to Samson quietly.

Samson looked at Logan and Chuck 'Savages,' he said. 'Every now and then they come by looking for something or somebody. Maybe snatch a child or woman if they can. We have the manpower, but they are surprisingly quick considering they are just rabid animals. The hunger turns them mad you see. We took one in once to see if we could feed him up and help get him mentally better. We kept him tied up as a precaution, nevertheless he escaped. But not before eating the guard.'

'We saw one on our way here. He killed our friend,' said Logan.

'It's very hard to defeat an army of monsters who don't care whether they live or die. We'll try to pick them off one at a time, but if they all get through our extra manpower won't have any advantage. They don't need weapons. If they get close enough it'll be like fighting a mountain lion. They know we're in here and they have the hunger, so they won't leave until they get what they want. We need to finish this now. Will you fight with us?' said Samson.

'Yes,' said Tallulah who was stood with the group behind Samson wielding various weapons. 'What do we do?'

'Take up a place that is well covered and shoot anything that comes through that door when we open it. They don't care about the dark and they have a strong sense of smell. When they come, they will come fast. Do not hesitate to put a bullet in them and do not think that they are human beings. They haven't been human for a long time,' said Samson.

The men at the gate started backing away and getting in a position to make contact, whilst the group scattered in pairs behind anything that served as a shield. Samson raised his hand and held it in the air for what seemed like ages, before dropping it. The gate clattered upwards and everything became a blur.

Logan watched what looked like a greyhound bound through the room on four legs and leap at one of the men headfirst. Before he knew it, the man was on the floor and the creatures face was covered in the man's blood. Seconds later a bullet ripped through the air and into the creature. Logan felt real fear for the second time, since he heard his father condemn half the country to death and then watched his friend ripped to pieces.

Gunfire rang out as more of these creatures, some dressed and some half naked rushed through the entrance. Some looked like vampires from old films he had seen. Pale and with glistening teeth and claws, but there was no doubt that these animals were once human.

Tallulah didn't know where to look. There was noise all around, whether it be the rat-a-tat of gunfire or the shrieks coming from the creatures. She held her gun tighter knowing she was the last line of defense and looked behind at the women and children huddled fifty yards behind her in the warehouse. It was absolute carnage and blood spilled across the warehouse floor as the men battled against these monstrosities, who had no issue with tearing strips of flesh from the men with their teeth. They looked like something from a horror film.

The fighting seemed to go on for ages until suddenly it was quiet again.

'How many left?' someone shouted.

'Seven,' came the reply.

The remaining creatures had got passed the first line of men and were hiding within the warehouse amongst the many tents and homes. Samson's men and the group of boys turned towards where Tallulah and Faye were standing and shuffled quietly towards them guns pointed at potential hiding places. Suddenly another shriek and one of the things, a bag of skin and bones launched itself towards Chuck and pinned him to the floor. It shook for a while before Chuck rolled over revealing his machete sticking from the creature's gut. 'Whoa now. Too close for comfort,' he said. 'I make that six left.'

'Arrrrrrrgh,' came the shout from Samson, as another Savage had jumped on his back and sunk its gnarly teeth into his shoulder. Samson swung around unable to reach it, his large arms flailing above his head. It grasped at his throat, as he managed to grab its head and wrestle it to the floor crushing its head into the ground. Blood oozed from his shoulder, but he dismissed it like it was nothing and held up his hand 'five.'

Tallulah blinked as she watched something moving towards the families. It was stood upright and fully dressed and it took a double glance to realize it wasn't one of the survivors. It looked almost normal, other than the dark piercing eyes, as it turned and smiled at her. More human than the others but somehow even scarier because of the fact it or he was closer to them in the scale of this messed up new world order. She walked towards him; her gun raised in front of her.

'Tals, what are you doing?' whispered Faye.

'He's going for the children,' she said moving forward with pace.

As Faye stepped forward to put a hand on Tallulah's shoulder to pull her back, two of the animals working as a pack took hold of Faye, one digging its claws into her abdomen and pulling her away into the shadows. Samson's men shot towards the area Faye had been taken, before Logan's voice was heard over the gunfire. 'Stop. Let us go in there and find them,' he pleaded.

Tallulah was in shock, but her attention came back to the one headed for the back of the warehouse. Tears rolled from her eyes thinking about Faye, but she wasn't about to let anyone else get killed. By now the creature was circling the children and eyeing up the potentially most delicious and filling meal, drooling at the thought of it. Tallulah lifted her gun. She was a few feet away as it turned around and faced her.

She'd never seen anything close to what she was looking at now. A real-life monster who was looking straight through her and into her soul as if it knew every little secret and didn't care who it told. It's eyes were sunken back and both eye sockets were black with dried blood around them. It smiled to revealed brown teeth like razor blades, easier to take down its prey quickly. That smile was one of a predator, who had no qualms about killing all and anything in front of it.

She raised her gun with both hands and pointed it towards the thing in front of her. But as she did the creature raised its hands up in surrender, inch long talons on every fingertip. Hands still up, the smile departed and instead a rather sad and pathetic human being stood in front of her. It opened its mouth and a noise from the back of his throat implored 'help me.' Her hands shaking, she slowly lowered her gun. As she did so, she felt a warm liquid cover her face as the Savage pounced at her and Logan simultaneously put a bullet through its chest.

Time had stood still but now frantically Logan took her by her hand 'Three left Tals and two of them have Faye.' They ran through the mass of shelters and tents looking for Faye.

Seth was stood by a tent his hand over his mouth when Tallulah and Logan reached him. Inside the tent the two creatures sat huddled over Faye obscuring her body. Seth was paralyzed watching as Faye mouthed the words '*kill me*,' to him. Logan raised his gun to the oblivious creatures, high on human flesh, and rained bullets from a machine gun into the tent killing everything in there. When he took his finger off the trigger he was out of ammunition and Tals sunk into him, her legs like jelly, sobbing uncontrollably.

'We've got it,' shouted Samson. Logan, Tallulah and Seth headed out to the opening where one of the creatures was hanging from a chain in the middle of the warehouse. 'Logan, I underestimated you and your team. I'm sorry for the loss of your friend. She seemed very nice. I was skeptical of what you were telling me, and I know I haven't been very forthcoming. I know you have your reservations about us, but I am not hiding anything from you. We have fought to survive this long and we live to fight until the next battle. We support your quest to find your Professor and thank you for what you are doing. You really are heroes. Tomorrow morning, we will escort you to the Police Station and the prison.'

'And what next for that monster,' said Logan.

One of Samson's men stood before him holding out a Samurai sword, which he drew from its sheath.

'Next, for this one, who was once my brother, peace,' and he bought the sword down slicing the creatures head from its body.

Next morning Samson kept to his promise and took the group the two-hour journey to the Police Station. The roads were quiet and despite Samson telling them that no-one would attack during the day they were still very aware of the preceding nights events and what had happened to Faye. All were on edge and Tallulah in particular was understandably upset at the loss of her friend.

'This is as far as we go my friend,' Samson said to Logan

Logan held out his hand and Samson took it and pulled Logan into him.

'Just be careful in there son. Don't go in guns blazing. Expect the unexpected,' Samson said.

Logan pulled his hand away sharply wondering whether this was some kind of threat. He had known early on that Samson hadn't told him the whole truth about the Prison and this backed that up.

'Thank you for your hospitality Samson. Until we meet again,' said Logan.

Samson bellowed out a laugh and turned and started walking away and the rest of his men turned and walked off into the distance of the city.

'We're on our own again now guys,' he said to the remaining group.

'Just how we like it,' said Chuck.

They entered the Police Station and split off, first checking that they were as alone as they hoped. The station was small but had offices spread throughout the main floor. Stairs led down to the cells, along with the entrance into the prison. Logan indicated to them to follow him downstairs and with his gun ready he moved forward.

The staircase was dark and the only light in the cells was coming from the stairwell. They took out their torches and lit the way ahead. Downstairs the cells doors were open and one by one the group bunched together behind Logan examining each cell and moving along to the end of the corridor. They reached the last cell and Logan peered around the door. A loud screech rang out and Logan jumped backwards into the rest of them causing everyone to scream and panic.

'Its fine it's fine,' Logan said, 'It's just a cat.'

'Holy cow Logan. I thought it was one of those things,' said Chuck 'Are you trying to give me a heart attack?'

Tallulah smacked Logan on the arm and the group started laughing, first slowly and then into raucous laughter. Even Logan broke a smile and then couldn't stop himself bursting out into tears of laughter. Gradually the moment passed, and they looked at each other under the lights of the torches and Logan snapped back into army mode. 'This is it guys. Time to save the world,' he said dramatically.

The tunnel entrance was at the end of the corridor and the metal door was ajar. It looked like it had previously been covered with a bookcase, which had been shifted aside, scratch marks on the floor. 'That makes things easier,' said Xander. They continued through the door and down another corridor which led to a junction. 'The schematics say we go right and two hundred yards up there should be an entrance to a stairwell that goes into the first floor of the prison. Then there should be a door that takes us into the maintenance room of the gantry,' said Logan. 'Right it is then,' said Chuck.

'Light. I can see light up ahead,' said Seth. The door to the maintenance room had a window and light shone through to the top of the stairwell.

Logan tried the door and it didn't budge at first. Chuck joined him pushing and the door moved about an inch. All of them started pushing and the door swung open with the group falling into the room on top of each other.

'Right,' said Logan getting off the floor and composing himself 'Now comes the hard part. For all we know the rest of the prison could be full of the vilest criminals to walk the face of the earth.'

'Way to sell it to us,' said Tallulah.

'Or it could be empty,' he said. 'Which means **our** mission is over.'

'Well when you put it like that,' Tallulah replied. 'Where now?'

Logan pointed upwards to the ceiling.

'Air-**con** system?' Chuck laughed. Logan nodded.

'We need to do this quickly and quietly. It'll give us the best view of the prison and if the Professor is in here then a bigger chance of finding him. It will be slow and uncomfortable, but if we do it right the risk will be lower of us getting caught.'

Logan was first up and then one at a time they climbed into the air conditioning shaft. It was a lot larger than they expected and at a crouch they could shuffle along quite easily. They came across the first vent, which opened into the top of a prison cell, but it was empty. Looking forward Logan could see that every five feet vents opened into more cells, so he knew they were heading in the right direction. He stopped short of the next vent and peered inside. At first he thought it was empty and was about to move on but then he saw a man move from below the vent into the middle of the cell. He turned and put a finger to his lips. '*So, the prison was inhabited*,' he thought to himself. The Professor could be alive. But this wasn't him and he knew he had to press on quickly. He turned again and held his hand down and whispered 'quietly,' to the rest of them.

Moving from vent to vent he saw more men, ranging from two to sometimes five, in each cell, either playing cards or board games. None of them looked unhealthy or starving to death though and he wondered if this was as a result of the cannibalism he had heard of and seen with his own eyes at Samson's camp. No sign of the Professor and they were coming to a bend in the air-con tunnel. They turned right again and continued along, peering into the cells, carefully trying to go unnoticed. Every now and then one of them would make a noise or cough and the group would stay deadly still until they knew they had gone undetected and then move on.

It felt like they had been in there hours and they had almost done a full perimeter of the first floor of the prison. Reaching the end of the unit Logan scrutinized the last vent. It was a room with tables and chairs in it. Not an office as such but more like a makeshift guard room. It had windows into the main prison, but they were whitewashed so that no-one could see in, or out. He pulled out the prison map he had and deliberated their next move.

'Tals,' he whispered. 'Looking at the map, if we climb down into this room, there is a stairwell next door which leads to the next floor up. We can then access the vent to the room directly above and do the next level. What do you think?'

'So once in the room we need to go out into the prison to get to the stairwell?' she replied.

'It's the only way to get to the next floor.'

'Then that's what we do,' she said.

He nodded and started removing the hatch to the room, dropping down and then helping the others down. He scanned the room diligently but quickly. 'Right,' he started saying to the group, ready to explain the plan. But before he could continue the door swung open and a man walked through the door, followed by more men with guns drawn. They had been caught.

CHAPTER THIRTEEN

The group were surrounded with the men's guns pointed at their heads. Logan nodded compliantly and lowered himself to the ground, his own gun out in front of him and laid it down looking to the others to do the same, which they dutifully did.

The door opened and a man covered in prison tattoos, whose head barely cleared the door frame, walked into the room. Almost unnoticeable behind this behemoth another man had also entered. Not as big but his presence seemed to fill the room. 'Mr Logan Mathers,' he said smiling.

Logan remained calm but wondered how he knew who he was. 'Television Ese,' the man said pointing to a screen up in the corner of the room, answering the unspoken question in Logan's eyes. The TV was silent, but he watched his father sat at his desk talking on a loop. 'There's not much to watch, but he has plenty to say. The photo on the desk. You, right? A little younger, no, but still your father's son. You of course know who I am, because that's why you're here.'

'Look Sir, just give me a minute to explain Mr. Mendez,' Logan said recognizing the ill-famed criminal

'Sshh,' he said putting his finger to his mouth 'It's been a long time since someone called me mister.' The men holding the guns at the group laughed among themselves. 'He said you would come, although I didn't think he would send children.' Mendez paced the room passing each person and staring them down. 'You are either very well trained or very lucky. Nobody has got in here since the food supplies started to run low.'

'Mr Mendez Sir, we are here to help you, we're looking for a man, a professor,' said Tallulah.

'Ah Princess, do we look like we need help? We know exactly who you are here for.' He motioned to one of the men nearest the door. 'obtener el professor.' Mendez looked back to the screen pointing at The President. 'A very clever man but surrounded with fools I'm afraid. Which are you Logan?'

Logan waited to see if he was expected to reply but just as he started to speak a man walk into the room, hands voluntarily behind his back. The man was looking down at the ground and talking to himself 'ah, Isaac, what have we here? Usurpers perhaps? Or are they assassins? Yes, assassins I believe. We have been expecting you. Please, please tell me why you are here, if not to do away with me?'

Tallulah stepped forward again 'Professor, you may not remember me.' The Professor looked up at her. 'Tallulah. It cannot be. Look at you, a woman no less. Do my eyes deceive me? But you have come here to kill me?'

'No Professor, we are here to help you. You are in danger.'

'I very much doubt that Princess,' Mendez spoke up. 'On the contrary, we are very much safe.'

'The President, my father, and the rest of the surviving government have made a plan to release a toxin into the water supply, which will kill over half of the remaining population. They will be completely oblivious that it has even happened until people start dying.'

'To what end? What purpose does this serve them?' said the Professor.

'The rate of the diminishing supplies against the remaining population means that humanity will be non-existent in months. They think by culling half of everyone left living that they stand a chance of rolling out sustainable living for the half of the population who live.'

'Ridiculous,' said the Professor 'On what grounds do they possibly think this will work?'

'No disrespect Sir, but this is based on years of research from people who know what they are talking about. Not some criminal who runs with Mexican Death squads,' Zack interjected, whilst the rest of them stared at him critically.

'Death Squads?' Mendez laughed 'What is a Death Squad?'

The other men in the room looked at each other bemused then one man said to another '*el escuadrón de la muerte*,' and they started laughing again.

Zack pulled a face 'Your Death squads who go out at night taking people off the streets,' he shrugged 'Cannibalism.' The men knew this word and laughed again.

'Why are you here Tallulah? Seriously. If not to kill me, what is it you seek?' said the Professor.

'Whether or not their plan works, they are going to use the toxin in the water supply. We need an antidote. You are the only person I know cleverer than my father who could do such a thing. We took a massive chance coming here not knowing whether you were even alive. We need your help.'

'What makes you think I am capable of such a thing? I have been in this place for years now, with no laboratories, nothing. What makes you think I want to help?'

'I still know the man you were. I remember when I was a little girl, you said to me '*if we are just a mistake and passing through this worlds life cycle then why make us individuals. The answer is simple, because as individuals we have the choice to make that life cycle better or worse. I will always choose better.*'

'Ah, choice. You are asking me to choose now of course.' the Professor mused. 'You of course have a sample of the toxin?'

'Yes,' Logan said.

'Are you really entertaining this Mr. Brittle?' said Mendez.

'So many questions today Isaac. It's about time we started to give some answers. Logan, Tallulah, please come with me, I have something to show you. Isaac, please can you make our other guests feel at home in the canteen.'

Mendez nodded and the other men lowered their guns and waved the group out of the room and down a grey hallway.

'Death Squads?' the Professor said to Mendez as he joined Logan and Tallulah.

'Hey, you see. They still have eyes on us. But sometimes the eyes lie. No?'

The Professor led the pair down a metal staircase and up to a large double door, a huge lock across the riveted four-inch-thick steel. As he opened the doors bright sunshine blinded them momentarily until their eyes adjusted to the light, revealing a farm before them. In the prison courtyard men were digging at the ground whilst another chased a chicken around, swearing in Spanish.

'Surprised?' Mendez said.

Logan looked at him 'How?'

The Professor smiled.

'You have to remember Mr. Mathers; we were not always criminals. Yes, we have done bad things in the past. I am very aware of the things I have done and when I make peace with my maker, I will accept his decision. I deserve to be locked up forever, but this man did not,' he held out his hand to the Professor.

'Thank you, Isaac, but others would disagree with you I am afraid. None more so than this man's father I am sure,' said the Professor.

'What do you mean? Why are you here? What did you do?' said Logan.

'More to the point, what didn't I do. But we shall get to that. Let us show you around,' said the Professor. 'We have corn, fresh tomatoes, potatoes, cabbages, carrots over there.'

'Don't forget chilies,' said Mendez.

'Of course, Isaac. Our Mexican compadres make up eighty percent of the casa de la nueva vida and they love their chilies.'

'House of New Life?' Logan translated.

'Yes Mr. Mathers. Every one of the people living within these walls was blessed with a new life. Not when The Cure came, but when the food stopped coming. We were the first to suffer and rightly so, but then we found out that we had a God living among us. A man of such knowledge that we would come to worship the ground he walked on, my good friend the Professor,' Mendez beamed.

'So melodramatic,' said the Professor.

'Mr Brittle had been in the prison four years and yet we had never crossed paths. He kept to himself, nonetheless it was clear he did not belong among us. The worst criminals the world had to offer lived here, but he was not one of them. However, when we needed him there he was. He taught us to grow crops where no crops could grow. He helped us find animals we could breed for farming. We have twelve pigs I think, no fourteen, goats, two cows and countless chickens now, but we started with nothing. Look at these men out here working together. Believe it or not some are guards who chose to stay rather than face the atrocities which awaited them outside. The bars are still here to keep people out, but unlike our President we did not forget the people outside our gates. The Death Squads you mentioned are my men taking food into the city and feeding those who cannot feed themselves. We have to keep them out so we can grow big enough to extend beyond the walls, which we will,' he looked to the Professor who nodded approval back.

'Nobody dies here. Nobody steals. We work together for the greater good. We work to do the very thing your father plans to take away from us, and that is to give the people a choice,' said the Professor.

'You did all this?' Tallulah said.

'No, we did all this. Every man within these prison walls is free to walk out whenever they want but they choose to stay, to live, and to help others live.'

'It may not be the luxury you have become accustomed to, but to us, this is paradise,' said Mendez.

'Actually, where we have been living is more like a prison than here,' said Logan.

The Professor led them back into the prison and into the kitchens where the smell of freshly cooked bread filled the air. More men scurrying around carrying pots, testing food and stirring steaming hot vessels of food. Logan and Tallulah had never seen anything like it.

'Apologies if my men give you any strange looks, but most haven't seen a woman in many years. Especially one so beautiful Princess. You are completely safe of course but forgive their stares,' said Mendez apologetically.

'Professor, you said you were put here for something you didn't do. Why?' said Tallulah, choosing to ignore Mendez' comment.

The two men looked at each other 'You don't know?' said Mendez.

'No, why would we?' said Logan.

'Well, for one you are The President's son, but she is Wanikiy's daughter,' said the Professor.

'What does that mean?' said Tallulah.

'Your father didn't tell you what caused The Cure?' he said.

'Something caused The Cure?' said Logan.

'Good Lord yes son, it wasn't divine intervention, it was me,' said Professor Brittle.

Logan and Tallulah couldn't believe what they were hearing and were speechless. This revelation was too much on top of everything they had heard, and Logan couldn't find the words to reply.

'You? You caused this?' said Tallulah.

'This?' said the Professor waving his hands in the air as Tallulah had. 'This being the end of the world, famine, death of humanity, the apocalypse? No. If I had then ending up in here would have been the least I deserved. No. Your father and I only created The Cure. We are not responsible for the repercussions.

'My father? He has never mentioned anything about this. The Cure, we thought, was something else, not man made,' said Tallulah.

'Yes, like the rest of the world, but I had thought that those privy to what the left hand of the President knows would know too. Maybe even that secret was too barbaric to share, like poisoning half the country, I guess.'

'Goldsmith?' said Logan.

'Yes, he was behind everything from the start. The government knew the scientists of the world were on the verge of discovery. Cures to Cancer, AIDS, Heart Disease, you name it, they were close. Some had already been discovered but were awaiting approval for testing on live subjects. The five largest Pharmaceutical companies knew it too and they knew that they would lose billions once the cures were made available to the masses. They couldn't pay off everyone, so they made a deal with the US Government to find a cure that was capable of curing and stopping anyone from ever getting ill in the future. It wasn't about saving lives, it was always about making money. Goldsmith instigated everything and his first move was bringing your father and I to find the magic cure.'

'But my father was trying to help people. He loved my mother and would do anything to stop people going through what we as a family had gone through. It was never about the money for him, it was about the guilt that he couldn't save her,' said Tallulah.

'As was I my dear Tallulah, but we were oblivious to Goldsmith's end game. Logan, your father was still Senator at the time, but his predecessor gave us carte blanche of everything at the Government's disposal. We had access to Area 51 and substances which we had no idea what they were or what they were capable of, but we used them anyway in our campaign for a cure. We thought we were saving mankind and that just drove us to take bigger chances and more risk.'

'But you did it. You found a cure to cure all illness. What went wrong?' said Logan.

'Yes, we found a cure, but not a way to administer it. The Government planned to sell the drug through the Pharmaceutical companies, but we couldn't get it into pill or liquid form. It was a gas which could be breathed in but there was no way it could be sold on the open market. And by the way, we are taking about gases that cannot even be found on planet Earth, that we had no idea if they had any long-term side effects. But Goldsmith was working to a deadline. The Pharmaceutical companies needed proof that it worked so Goldsmith set up an experimental test on a town just outside of Mississippi with a population of less than four thousand people. Out of those four thousand people two hundred of them had been involved in an asbestos poisoning accident, so for Goldsmith this was the perfect way to show them the cure worked. We went over those figures a thousand times and by having planes release the gas over the town it had a target area of five square miles. It should have gone airborne throughout the town and in theory cured anyone within the area of any illness they might have. Despite what the figures told us we were dealing with, Wanikiy and I were concerned about releasing that much gas, which had never been done. Goldsmith ignored me and your father and went ahead with the test. As soon as the gas was released and entered the atmosphere it started to expand at a rate we hadn't seen. Within seconds our apparatuses were going off the charts as it spread outside of the town and continued growing. It could have easily killed everyone and everything. Instead the Cure completely covered the whole planet within hours, curing everyone in its path.

Nobody spoke.

'The,' Logan stopped. 'Alien gas?'

'Si, sounds loco Ese,' Mendez laughed 'Yet here we are?'

'Not exactly aliens my friend, but something we shouldn't have taken so lightly,' said the Professor. 'It was a mistake on a scale never seen before. Of course, the Pharmaceutical companies were taken care of by the Government and the whole thing was covered up. I was taken into a room and Goldsmith asked me whether I could be trusted. I made the mistake of letting my feelings be known and that we should share what we knew so we could prepare against any side effects, but Goldsmith had other ideas and I was buried deep in a place where nobody would believe me if I even wanted to tell them. After a few weeks when I wasn't joined by Wanikiy

I guessed that he had made a different choice to me and the fact that you now stand before me confirms it. Logan, if it's any consolation your father knew nothing of the experiment or what we were doing. As far as he is concerned The Cure was a natural event and when his predecessor committed Hari Kari, he was left with his legacy to clear up.'

'This is too much to take in,' said Tallulah.

'It was a mistake? All this time and it was a mistake,' said Logan.

'Take a minute,' said Mendez. 'It's a lot to process.'

Logan had so many questions to ask but Tallulah was his priority now. She was conflicted as to whether her father had been a victim or become the villain in everything Professor Brittle had just told them. Truthfully, she just wanted to break down and cry. He was also aware that the whole reason they were there in the first place was the mission to stop the government making another huge mistake. A mistake which would undoubtably affect the professor and his fellow prisoners first-hand.

They had come full circle back to the canteen where the rest of the group were sat chatting to the other prisoners, sharing tales and even jokes. They approached the others who all stood, as Logan and Tallulah were visibly shaken from what they had just heard. 'Everything ok Boss?' said Chuck to Logan.

Logan wasn't sure he had the answer to that question, but he smiled and nodded. Mendez put a hand on his shoulder 'Well, at least we now know you are not here to kill anyone,' he laughed.

The laughter was short lived as he heard a gun cock and turned around to see Zack holding his gun against the Professors head 'They may not be here to kill anyone, but I've got other plans.'

Chapter Fourteen

Danny pulled up to the trellis gates of the reservoir, which were hanging off as though something had hit them at force. The place was silent, and he walked the motorbike into the forecourt of the reservoir and removed the contents from the box on the back, throwing up the C4 and catching it again, before stopping himself and considering the consequences of dropping that little block of explosives. He could hear the whooshing of the water now, although he couldn't see it and he closed his eyes and breathed in the fresh air before exhaling and walking towards the entrance to the building.

It looked like any office building on the inside, minus the people rushing around and the fact that the reception was unmanned. He pulled out the diagrams that he had for the buildings and looked around for the entrance to the underground walkway which housed the main water system.

A loud beep sounded, and Danny jumped. Then an automated voice.

'You are trespassing on government property. Please leave the building.'

'You are trespassing on government property. Please leave the building.'

Although technology had progressed massively in the last twenty years, Danny hadn't seen outside of the base for years, and whilst he knew artificial intelligence was in place as a security measure, he wasn't sure exactly what to expect. 'I swear, if there are 'replicants' here it's game over,' he said to himself recollecting his entire experience of artificial intelligence from the films he had watched.

Danny followed the blueprints and passed the front desk and down some stairs to an area which was open plan with desks lined up in a semi-circular fashion in front of a giant screen. The screen flicked between security footage of the reservoir and a broadcast every thirty seconds of his father warning everyone to evacuate and move to safe and secure areas of the country. He stood there looking at the ten-foot-tall vision of his father and nodded 'I hope I'm doing you proud Dad.'

He lifted his haversack and walked between the desks to the door at the back of the room. Looking through the window he jumped backwards as a face appeared behind the glass. 'A hologram,' he said to himself as the face peered back at him. 'Name and security code?' a voice came through the speaker on the wall. 'Erm, Daniel Mathers,' he stammered. 'Not recognized,' came the reply. He had not been prepared for this and he started to become flustered. He grabbed a nearby chair and threw it at the door. 'Name and security code?' came the voice again. 'President Nathanial Mathers,' he said. 'Not recognized,' repeated the hologram with no expression on its face. Danny picked up the chair he'd just thrown and sat down on it looking for inspiration.

In the silence, weighing up his options, Danny heard a noise from upstairs. He jumped up startled and ran over to the entrance to the room. He contemplated climbing the stairs and confronting whatever had made the noise, but he thought twice. He secured the doors with a broken chair leg through the door handles, wondering if it would hold.

Running back to the security door he looked chillingly into the dead eyes of the hologram looking back at him 'Name and security code?' Frustrated, and almost in tears that he had come so far and was now not going to be able to complete his mission, he rested his arms and head against the door, completely exhausted. As he did, the door moved open. 'Override effected,' came the voice again as Danny almost fell through the door. Composing himself he walked through the door and past the hologram cursing. Now he had a choice to make. Did he close the door behind himself and ensure no-one else followed him inside, but risk not being able to get out again, or leave it open and hope the noise he had heard was nothing?

He left the door ajar and walked forward into a tunnel. It had reinforced windows overlooking a lake thirty feet below and solid steel structures on the right of him. The walls were cold and damp to the touch and he could feel the movement of water down the other side despite a good two meter thickness to the wall. If he had placed the C4 here it would make no impact whatsoever. He needed to find the weak point and attach the explosives. Time was a concern and he hadn't heard anything through the walkie-talkie for some time. The not knowing what was happening with Logan was far worse than being here with the world on his shoulders.

Moving along the tunnel it opened out every ten feet and a monitor above him broadcast the message from his father, 'find a safe area.' 'I gave up my safe area Dad, to save your ass,' he said begrudgingly.

Ahead of him he could see a tent pitched up against the side of the tunnel. He slowly approached it and looked inside. A skeleton still inside a sleeping bag was the only occupant. He looked around at the possessions around the tent and picked up some photos and flicked through them. Empty tins of food scattered around. Someone obviously saw this as a safe area but failed to consider their ongoing food source. Danny felt sad that this person had died alone with nothing but their memories.

Up ahead he saw the walls curve inwards and there was a metal framed vault door within the wall. This was it. A small port hole in the vault door showed nothing but water falling from above. 'Right,' said Danny, mentally preparing himself for what he needed to do.

****

Back at the prison Zack's gun pressed against the Professor's head, leaving a red mark against his temple, whilst the others watched on. Mendez edged ever closer towards the boy, but Zack was watching every move.

'Seriously, you think I can't see you?' he said to Mendez.

'Look Zack, whatever this is about, we can sit down and talk about it,' said Logan.

'Time for talking is over. Did you really think your little plan was going to work? They've known about your little gang of ungrateful losers since pretty much the beginning,' said Zack.

Logan looked at the others to see if they knew anything about what he was saying but the blank faces said it all.

'Really? You think they knew anything about it. None of them had a clue. Not even Faye, may she rest in peace. Ha-ha. Jay, yes,' he smiled 'that was

MacGregor and me. Don't worry, he didn't feel a thing. Ha-ha. Went down like a sack of spuds. Goldsmith told me to keep an eye on you after they had the initial meeting to put everything into place. He knew not to trust you. He said you were weak and that you would find a way to mess up any chance of a future.' His finger on the trigger started to twitch.

'We knew exactly what you were up to down to the last detail. Goldsmith said you'd come here. Although to be fair he thought our good Professor here would be long gone. That was the whole point of putting him with the worse human beings in the world. But here we all are,' he chuckled.

'And your plan was to what? Shoot the Professor and walk out of here alive?' said Mendez.

'Something like that,' said Zack 'I'm thinking more of a hostage situation to be honest. I hadn't thought that far ahead,' he snorted.

'So, Goldsmith didn't trust me? That's interesting,' said Logan 'I'm a little distrusting myself if I'm honest. I mean like Jay just slipping like that. Sounded a bit fishy to me. You just turning up and finding him. Now you got to know that felt off to me,' Logan started walking towards Zack.

Zack started to feel a bit nervous and waved Logan away with the gun.

'I've got no problem taking you out soldier boy. This is my destiny man. Save mankind.'

'Hey, you know what, it's almost like you think I didn't know Goldsmith was going to have me watched. Trust is a two-way thing. That's why I trusted everyone in this team, except you. That's why I gave you an unloaded gun back at the base,' said Logan.

Zack froze like a rabbit in headlights and pointed the gun towards Logan's chest. But Logan kept walking towards him. 'You're bluffing,' he said.

'Are you asking me or telling me?' Logan smiled until the gun was now pressed against him

'How? How did you know? You're lying.'

'Truth is I wasn't sure back at the base about you. I had my doubts then. However, it wasn't until Jay came around about half hour ago and contacted us on the satellite phone that I knew everything. He told me the last thing he saw was you in the reflection of a mirror in his room standing behind him.'

'You're lying,' he panicked.

'Why don't you pull the trigger and find out.'

'Logan, no,' said Tallulah.

Click. The gun went silent. Click, click, click. Nothing.

Two of Mendez's men ran towards Zack and pushed him to the floor his hands behind his back.

'Very clever Mr. Mathers,' said the Professor 'Maybe I should give you more credit for this plan after all. You seem to have thought of everything.'

'If there's one thing I knew I could count on it was Goldsmith finding out what we were doing. He knew I'd struggle with the decision to use the toxin, and I knew he would send someone after me. I thought it would be McGregor though. Which means chances are he's been sent after Danny. We need to let him know. What you going to do with Zack?' he looked at Mendez.

'If there is one thing we have in bountiful supply it is prison cells. Take him away,' he motioned to his men who dragged Zack away, his legs flailing on the floor.

'Jay also told me that our father has given the order to send the toxin to the reservoir. They will be there within two days. If Danny is still alive, we need to get him to put everything in place in case you can't deliver an antidote,' said Zack.

'Logan, I hate to tell you this but the chances of me being able to create an antidote are slim. Given the circumstances and my limited access to any chemicals I don't know if I can find an antidote in the next ten years, let alone two days,' said the Professor.

'We don't have two days,' Tallulah spoke up 'We've got less. I'm going back to the base and I'm going to get them to either change their minds or get a message out to the rest of the country not to drink the water,' she pointed up at the television in the corner of the room.

'Tallulah, no. I don't want you going back. We need you here,' said Logan.

'Ah, Logan, you obviously do not know the Wanikiy stubbornness,' the Professor said perceptively.

'I've got to do this Logan. I need to right my father's mistakes.'

'But how will you even get back to the base?' said Logan.

Mendez stepped forward and waved out an arm 'perhaps I can help with that. Follow me.'

Following Mendez along the prison corridors, Logan and Tallulah filled in the rest of the group with what they had been told about The Cure and how it had been orchestrated by the government. In between gasps and Chuck's 'goddamns' Mendez led them to the very back of the prison to two massive rear exit gates.

'Through here my friend,' said Mendez.

The double door opened, and sun shone through them blinding them. Their eyes adjusted onto a huge airfield of around twenty airplanes ranging from small light aircraft to a military cargo plane.

'Goddamn,' said Chuck.

'Goddamn indeed, although it was not God who got these planes,' said Mendez.

'This is amazing,' said Logan. He looked at Tallulah. 'you got to do this right?' She nodded.

'One problem,' said Mendez. 'We have lots of planes, but not so many pilots.'

'But you do have **a** pilot?' said Logan.

'Mmmm. Yes. Kind of,' replied Mendez.

'Kind of?'

'He can be a little grumpy. He's over there by the gates.'

Everyone turned to the gates, but no-one could see anyone. They shrugged their shoulders looking at each other. 'Over there,' Mendez pointed towards some broken crates and old potato sacks.

'Hod! Come, meet our new friends. I have a mission for you,' said Mendez.

The sacks moved and what looked like a man on his knees held his arm up to shield the sun from his face.

As they watched the man it became apparent that he was not on his knees, but he was stood a full three feet and change tall. Not only was he a dwarf but he had a patch over his eye.

'A one-eyed dwarf?' said Chuck to Mendez.

Mendez shrugged 'I think the term is one eyed midget.'

'This is crazy,' said Logan. 'You expect this man to fly Tallulah across the country in a plane.'

'Very good pilot Mr. Mathers,' said the Professor 'He made many flights across the border and hardly ever crashed, isn't that right Hod?'

The dwarf looked Tallulah up and down 'Humph. I waited in this hovel ten years for a woman and you bring me a giant.'

'She's here to help save the world Hod and she needs your help,' said Mendez.

'Is he drunk?' quizzed Chuck.

Mendez held his hand up and moved it from side to side 'maybe a little. He flies better that way.'

'You're going to let him fly you back to the base?' said Logan.

'Do we have a choice?' said Tallulah, as Logan passed her a vial with half the toxin in it.

Hod smiled at them both.

They climbed into the small military fighter plane, Hod now wearing a Viking helmet in the front of the cockpit and a nervous looking Tallulah in the back. 'wait,' said the Professor. He took a step closer to the airplane and looked at Tallulah 'Your family name. Wanikiy. You know what it means?'

'Yes. It means Savior,' she replied.

'Your father once thought that it was prophecy that he would cure all the illness in the world. He was right. But it wasn't because of a name. It was because he thought he was above everyone else and it backfired. Maybe that prophecy was true, but it wasn't for him,' he smiled, took her hand, kissed it and waved goodbye.

'So, Savior,' said Hod 'are you ready for the ride of your life?'

'What were you in prison for?' Tallulah shouted through to the cockpit.

'Drug smuggling for the cartels. Would've got away with it though, but I ran out of fuel above a military airbase. Weeeeeeee, bang,' he mimicked a plane falling from the sky.

The others watched on as Hod attempted to start the plane, then again, then again.

'Third times a charm,' he winked, barely able to look out the window.

The plane stuttered and stumbled along the makeshift runway and straining the wheels lifted off the ground and gradually began to climb up and up. Then she was gone.

'Professor. It's time,' said Logan.

The group retreated back into the prison and to the Professor's laboratory which doubled as the infirmary. As they entered, they knew then why the professor had been skeptical about an antidote. The laboratory was mainly full of plants and looked nothing like the high-tech labs back at the base.

The sole reason for this laboratory had been to look at ways of self-sustainability and ways that they could fuel the prison and find new and different ways to grow food. What wasn't there to help long-term growth of the prison was day to day medicine to treat minor illnesses from before The Cure. The team looked at each other concerned and both the Professor and Mendez picked up on it straight away.

'I'm sorry Logan. I'm not sure what you were expecting. This is a prison,' said the Professor.

'I know Sir. It's fine. I knew it was a long shot.'

'Give me the rest of the Toxin and let me see what I can do,' he said.

An hour passed and all the group were spaced around the laboratory listening to the Professor clatter around with test tubes and other laboratory kit, but no shouts of Eureka. Nobody spoke and most had their head in their hands.

'Is there anything we can do to help,' said Xander, who had run out of cigarettes and had moved on to prison rollups that he'd scrounged off inmates.

'No son, sorry, no luck and no ideas of what he has used. Whatever he has put in this it is diluted so much that it's almost impossible to split into separate chemicals,' said the Professor.

'Just keep trying Professor. You're our only hope,' said Scott.

The professor looked over the top of his glasses 'aren't you the ray of sunshine?' he laughed.

****

Meanwhile Hod was giving Tallulah a running commentary of everything they passed over, but she couldn't hear a word. The flight would take about four hours and she now had to work out how she would get back into the base without being seen and into the communications room. She had a plan, but it would be costly and right now with tears in her eyes she couldn't think about it. She wiped them away and gritted her teeth, sat up straight and listened to the half blind dwarf flying the plane.

****

Logan had been trying to get hold of Danny for a couple of hours with no luck. The radio crackled and spluttered but nothing from his brother. Jay had given them a heads up, but it wasn't looking good on all fronts. The Professor was out of his depth without the necessary equipment and with Tallulah gone hope was fading fast. The radio crackled and a voice spoke.

'Lo....Lo....over,' came the voice.

'Danny. Is that you, over?'

Lo…. Logan? Logan,' came Danny's voice.

'Danny, can you hear me? Over.'

'Thank goodness, I've been trying to get hold of you Logan. McGregor....Over.'

'Yes Danny, we know. Jay told us. Goldsmith sent Zack after us and McGregor after you. Over.'

'Are you all ok Logan? Did you find the Professor? Is Tallulah ok? Over.'

'We have the professor, he's alive. He's working on an antidote, but it doesn't look good. Over.'

'And Tallulah? Over.'

Logan paused.

'She's fine Danny, she's helping the Professor. Over,' he lied.

'Good good. I think McGregor is dead. I'm at the reservoir and at the vault. Over.'

'Jay says that they are sending the toxin now. They are already on their way. You have maybe a day and a half if we're lucky. You need to set those explosives. Over.'

'OK Bro, I'm on it. How long do I give it until I blow it? Over.'

'Leave it until you hear from me or the second one of those soldiers come walking through that door. Then get out. Over.'

'I hear you. I'll be in touch. Love you man. Over and out.'

'Love you too Danny. Over and out.'

The radio crackled to nothingness at Logan's end. Then the silence was broken with shouts from the laboratory. Logan ran back into the room.

'We may have found something,' said the Professor.

CHAPTER FIFTEEN

Hod lay back on his sun lounger, rays of heat shining down on his face from the blistering sun above the Mediterranean Sea and the forty-foot yacht slowly cutting its way through the water. He held a Cuban cigar in one hand and not far from his other was a cocktail on a table laden down with exotic fruit. Life could not get much better he thought, and he turned to look at the bikini clad supermodel on the lounger next to him. He smiled and picked a grape from the table, popping it in his mouth and nodding appreciably to the female waitress who had just bought him another drink.

But for all this Hod felt that something wasn't completely right, and he heard a far and distant voice in his head calling his name 'Hod, Hod.' He furrowed his brow trying to make out the voice and where it was coming from but looking back around, he decided that he was far too content in his current surroundings to be bothered.

In the back of the airplane Tallulah slammed her hand against the glass partition between her and the cockpit. 'Hod, Hod, wake up, wake up.' Hod awoke with a jump to see, with his one good eye, the ground hurtling towards him at two hundred miles an hour. 'arrrrrgh.' he yelled pulling at the controls in front of him and bringing the aircraft back to a level less concerning. 'It's fine it's fine, I wasn't asleep. I was just taking us down out to avoid any turbulence,' he said. Tallulah mumbled under her breath 'asshole.'

'Not long now Missy, maybe thirty minutes or so. Hope you've got a plan.'

'You just worry about getting us there in one piece and I'll worry about the plan,' she said.

Minutes passed and she could make out the town above the base. She wondered whether they were watching the plane. Surely everyone on the base would now know what they had done. Maybe Goldsmith had kept it to himself, in the hope that no-one else on the base ever found out of the plan to release the toxin. Only time would tell and Hod had begun the descent.

'Over there, away from the town, we'll walk in from a couple of miles away,' she said.

'Walk? I don't think so. Once we're down that as far as I go. I'll wait with the plane but any signs of trouble and I'm outta here.'

'Thanks, you're a real hero.'

'I'd wait until we've landed before you start calling me names,' he said.

As the aircraft got closer to the ground Hod started saying something that sounded like the Lord's Prayer, before the wheels touched the floor and he put the brakes on. Finally, the plane came to a stop and Hod crossed his chest and breathed a sigh of relief 'Landing was never one of my fortes.'

'Neither is staying awake, apparently.' she said with contempt in her voice. 'Stay here.'

Hod saluted.

As Tallulah got closer to the base she begin to panic. The exits were always manned, and she had no reason to believe today would be any different. She decided that the best course of action was to walk up and knock on the door as if nothing had happened. Not the most intricate plan, but a plan all the same. Yes, there would be questions, but once she was in, she could break away and get to the communications room. Once inside she could get the message out to anyone with access to a television of the plan to poison the water system.

As it was, she didn't even need to knock as two soldiers, one male and one female, came out to greet her. Saying nothing they both took an arm and frog marched her back into the base. She realized that she had made a grave mistake in returning alone and that she would most likely be bought in front of the President to answer some burning questions then thrown into the base confinement.

'What's going on,' she asked the soldiers. 'Where are you taking me?' Neither answered.

Led through the underground tunnels around the base and not through the main halls they didn't pass another person. 'Where is everyone? You can't do this to me.' They stopped at a door.

'Where are we? What are you going to do to me?' she pleaded, but nothing.

The soldiers released their grip on her and the male solider took out a key card and touched it against the electronic lock of the door. It beeped and the light went red. Again, a beep and then red. The solider shook his head and bent down to inspect the lock. As he did the female solider bought a cosh down on his head and he slumped to the floor out cold.

'We don't have much time,' said the woman. 'My name is Rose, and I know all about the plan the government have to kill everyone. I don't have time to explain everything, but I will once everything has worked itself out. I'm guessing you need to get to the communications room?'

'Ahem,' she nodded, completely unaware of what was going on.

'Follow me. We can go through this way. Most of the others have been deployed to take the toxin across country to the reservoir. Are the others still alive?' she said.

'Others?' Tallulah asked.

'Logan, Danny, the others.'

'Yes, yes, well I think so. They were when I left. Who are you?'

'It'll all become clear but I'm just someone who agrees that what you are doing is right. The President may not see it, but there's many people on this base who will. You must tell them. You must make them see that it's not our right to decide for another person. Especially one like this. Now, we have to go.'

Tallulah followed the woman, Rose, having to double step to keep up every now and again as she was led around the tunnels. 'Through there,' said Rose. 'I can't take you any further, but I'll see you on the outside.'

'The outside?' said Tallulah.

'Trust me,' said Rose and she put her cap on Tallulah's head and her jacket over her shoulders.

Tallulah opened the door and she was suddenly in familiar surroundings. To her left were the stores and she thought of Brad Junior and doubt crept into her mind once again. Past the stores were the laboratories and if her memory served her right the communications room was somewhere past that, though she had never been there before. She kept her head down as a man walked around the corner 'Morning,' he said, but she just kept walking. 'Rude,' she heard the man say as he walked away.

The stores were busy as always, but so busy no-one even looked up at her, more concerned about the food stocks than a girl in army fatigues it would seem. The laboratories were next, and the doors were all safely locked. She passed her father's lab, but he was nowhere to be seen. Had he gone with the men to release the toxin. No, she didn't think so. The communications room was empty as expected and the door had a keypad rather than a key card. She stood there frozen not knowing the number combination, one finger poised out in front of her. As she stood there, she heard a noise and man stood almost next to her looking down at her and an angry sneer on his face '1776,' he said.

'I'm sorry?' she said.

'1776. The code to get in,' the man repeated.

'Oh, thank you,' she replied, 'I'd forget my own head if it wasn't screwed on.'

The man smiled and walked away.

Inside the room was a desk. The same desk she has seen on the television at the prison. She turned around and shut the door, locking it from the inside and went and sat at the chair behind the desk. 'Now what?' she wondered. She removed the rest of the toxin she had brought back with her and stared at it almost waiting for it to do something. 'You're the key, aren't you?' she spoke to the test tube.

Leaving it on the desk she moved over to the equipment and started switching buttons to ON. Before long the camera started whirring and she could see the desk on a monitor. She stood behind the desk.

Looking deep into the camera she started to speak.

****

Back at the reservoir Danny had pinpointed the weak spot in the center of the main reservoir dam and was setting up the explosives. He couldn't believe that he'd made it this far and was about to blow up one of the largest water filtration systems in the world, let alone America, but this is what it had come down to.

He knew that the army were on their way there with enough toxin to kill half the population and he knew that it was down to him to ensure that didn't happen. He tied together two wires and flicked a switch on the bomb. 'Time to rock and roll,' he said to himself.

'I wouldn't be so sure about that,' said McGregor, walking along the corridor towards him.

'It had to be you didn't it?' said Danny.

'Aye lad, only one man for the job I'm afraid.'

'I thought you'd died back out there.'

'So did I. It sure felt like it Danny boy.'

'So, what happens next?' said Danny.

'It can go two ways son. The first way is that you can switch off that little button there, walk over to me and we can go back to the base and let the good soldiers do their job. You get told off by your daddy and we get to live to a ripe old age,' said McGregor.

'And the other way?' said Danny, already knowing the answer.

McGregor drew his pistol 'I can come over there and switch it off myself, but I leave here alone.'

'But there is a third way,' said Danny and he held the detonator out in front of him, his thumb pressed tightly down on the red button on the top 'I'm guessing you know how this works.'

'Yes son, but you and I both know that explosive has a denotation area of about a hundred feet. Am I wrong? You take your finger off that button and it's not just the dam that goes Boom.'

'You think one life given isn't worth saving millions? I also get to take you with me McGregor.' he smiled.

'I don't think you've got the guts boy,' McGregor started walking forward again, gun drawn on Danny.

Then he stopped again. Monitors all-round the corridor of the reservation started to make white noise and black and white pixels started to become a desk. Both McGregor and Danny looked up at the monitor above McGregor's head.

Tallulah came onto the screen.

'Hello. If you are hearing this then I need to tell you that you are in grave danger. My name is Tallulah Wanikiy and I have been living on a government base for over ten years with the President and some of his closest aides and confidantes. We have lived well whilst you have suffered from starvation. Now the government have decided that the only way this life can continue is by taking away the lives of people so that the remainder of us can thrive. They intend to put a poison into the water system which will go out to most of the major cities and kill anyone who drinks it.'

Throughout the cities people watched Tallulah on their TV's. Some watched in their homes whilst others watched on giant screens in the streets. Everywhere in the country that still had electricity and access to a television, and who had been watching the same apocalyptic messages of hope from the President, were now watching an eighteen-year-old girl telling them that they would be murdered. There was silence everywhere and gasps from the people watching Tallulah give them the news that not only was help not coming, but they were expendable too. Human beings, some who hadn't eaten in weeks, bodies wasted away, faces like skeletons stared at this girl holding onto every word she spoke.

McGregor looked at Danny and then back to the screen. Danny's eyes had not left the screen since Tallulah had started speaking. He wanted to know what she would say next.

'I'm sorry for the crimes of our fathers. They truthfully think that what they are doing is right, but they are wrong. When The Cure happened, we were put in a position that we couldn't have known was coming. We rejoiced in something amazing as we watched our loved ones become well again. We forgot the other things that are important. The basic principles of life. But for that we can be forgiven. I have seen someone I love taken away from me because of an insidious disease that got inside her and slowly turned her into a different person. Everything I held dear about her drained out of her as this horrid wicked disease spread throughout her body. I do not judge anyone who had seen another human being go through this or any other disease rejoice in seeing them fit and healthy. But now know that we face that uncertainty again. We have turned against one another, whether it be on the streets fighting for food, or as a government against the people that we vowed to keep safe.'

****

Goldsmith and the President stood in the meeting room watching everything unfold on the giant screen above the very table they made the decision that led to Tallulah's stand. 'Get her out of there,' Goldsmith waved away two soldiers. As they left the room, Wanikiy walked in 'I knew nothing about this,' he said.

'Does it matter?' said Goldsmith 'The damage is done.'

'Shall I stop the soldiers delivering the toxin,' said Wanikiy,

'Yes,' said the President.

'No' said Goldsmith 'The plan goes ahead as normal. Not everyone will believe her and not everyone will see this communication. The plan goes ahead.'

****

Tallulah sat down at the desk. 'But now more than ever we must turn to the person next to us and call them brother or sister, because we are all that is left and we're family. We can get through this together, but it won't be easy. We have spoken to people out there who can sustain a normal healthy life and put food back on the table. We can grow as a nation again, but we must trust each other and the only way we can do that is by showing that we will do whatever is necessary to give you back your lives. Your government may have failed you, but we will not and the only way I can prove to you what I am saying is true is by making a sacrifice for you. In this test tube is an undiluted amount of the toxin they plan to put into the water that you drink to survive'.

Tallulah placed the test tube to her lips, closed her eyes and swallowed back the toxin.

As McGregor saw her ingest the poison on the monitor he turned to Danny and started to run towards him 'Nooooo!'

But it was too late. Danny closed his eyes and the detonator fell to the floor.

CHAPTER SIXTEEN

31st December 2020 - 11.02 pm - George Washington University Hospital

'Breathe Mrs. Mathers, breathe,' said the nurse sucking and blowing out her mouth in time with the lady on the hospital bed.

'It's fine Honey. Just take it easy,' said her husband by her side.

'If you tell me take it easy one more time Nathaniel J Mathers, I will take this oxygen tank and stick it where the sun don't shine,' said the man's wife.

'OK, OK,' he said, as she gripped his hand leaving nail marks in it as he pulled away.

Another man put his head around the door and beckoned to Nathanial.

'Senator Mathers can I have a word?' said the man.

'Really Nathanial? You can't just take one day away from the office. Let alone having one of your minions poking his head round the door looking at your wife in a hospital gown every five minutes,' said Brianna Mathers, wife to the Senator.

All the time a young boy sat in the corner of the hospital room reading his comic only occasionally looking up to see what the noise was about. All he knew was that he was getting a baby brother or sister and that surely meant he would have a new friend to play with.

'Five minutes Brianna, I'll be right back,' said the Senator.

He gladly left the room and rubbed his hand until the nail marks disappeared 'What is it Cole? What is so important you must interrupt me whilst my wife if about to give birth. This is supposed to be one of the most important moments of a man's life watching his children being born and here I am talking to you about what? How many times the bins get collected each week? When the May Day parade will take place?'

'Actually' said Cole 'I've got the president on the phone for you.'

'Oh,' said senator Mathers 'Well why didn't you say so? Give me the phone,' and he grabbed it out of his assistants hand. 'Mr President. How can I help you this evening? Rather late to be calling isn't it? Everything ok?'

The voice on the phone was cold and not at all emotive 'Senator, we're in the process of testing a new enhanced chemical drug which could revolutionize medicine in the future and I've been informed by the seven heads of my table that we need your sign off as it's within your state.'

Senator Mathers paused. It seemed strange to him that The President should require his sign off on anything. He'd never been required to agree any legislation before so why now. With that said it sounded like a breakthrough in the medical field and surely that could only be a good thing, right? 'Yes, Mr. President, you have my agreement. Please let my office know your findings and the outcome. Good luck,' he said.

'Senator, for the purposes of this call, which is being recorded, I need you to say the following for the record '*I, Senator Mathers, agree the use of chemical testing for the purposes of curing multiple disease and illness as proposed by the CDC in the state of Idaho on 31st December 2020,*' the President said over the telephone.

'Erm, ok, yes,' and the Senator repeated the message. 'Is there anything you're not telling me Mr. President,' he said jokingly.

'No Mathers, thank you for your time. I believe you're currently in Washington with your family. Please, give your wife my best and congratulations on your impending arrival,' he said stoically.

The phone went dead and the Senator tried to process what had just happened. He shook his head and went back into the hospital room.

When he opened the door, his wife was on her side and a doctor was injecting something into her back whilst two nurses looked on. One of the nurses had her hand on her mouth looking upset which immediately concerned him. 'What happened?' he said.

'It's fine, she started seizing,' said the doctor 'It's normal under the circumstances but we need to ensure her heart rate is kept at a minimum.'

'Under the circumstances? You mean giving birth?'

'No Senator, I mean with your wife's heart condition. Your first son was a normal birth?' said the doctor.

'No, yes, I mean, yes normal. He was pretty much out by the time we got to the hospital suite. It all happened so quick. Wait, heart condition? My wife doesn't have a heart condition,' said Mathers.

'It's right here in her charts Senator Mathers, since birth, and these pills,' he held up a small pot of tablets.

'For indigestion,' he said.

'No, for her heart sir. She has atherosclerosis, a blockage of her heart valves. If we do not manage the regulation of her heart it could have very serious consequences.'

'I didn't know, she never told me. Is she going to be ok? Is the baby ok?' said the senator.

The boy, Logan, peered over his comic taking everything in his stride. Nothing to see here he thought.

'I'm going to want to get an ultrasound in here to check the baby's heartbeat. Your wife is stable, but she's medicated. Once she becomes conscious you will need to calm her down and keep her breathing normally,' said the doctor.

'Yes, yes, ok, just tell me what to do.'

One of the nurses reassuringly put a hand on his shoulder whilst the other left the room, presumably to get the Ultrasound machine. The Senator was in shock that his wife had kept her heart problem a secret from him for so long and hearing that she had had a seizure had scared him. 'Logan, are you ok?' he said to his son. 'Yes dad,' the toddler replied without looking up.

The nurse returned with the Ultrasound machine and the doctor started rubbing ultrasound gel onto the machine and holding it on Brianna's stomach, moving left, then right, up and down, all the time squinting at the screen but not saying anything.

'Doctor?' the Senator almost pleaded with him.

'It's not good news I'm afraid Sir. Your baby seems to have the same heart condition. Its heartbeat is irregular. There's a very large possibility that the child's heart will not be strong enough to cope with the trauma of a normal birth. However, a caesarean will undoubtedly cause your wife the same stress on her heart. You will need to make a decision on how you want to proceed?'

The Senators legs felt like jelly underneath him. 'You mean I need to choose between my wife or my baby living?' His face turned red and he started sweating profusely. He wanted to be sick. 'Save my wife,' he said.

The doctor nodded that he understood.

The Senator's wife's eyes rolled back into her head and then back again and she started talking quietly. Nathanial held her hand, now limp, and rubbed it with his thumb. He felt a tear roll down his face as the doctor and nurse placed their hands within her gown and together started to try and take out the baby. He looked up at the clock in the room. The minute hand was suspended five minutes to midnight and the Senator tried to justify his decision to himself, wondering what he would tell Brianna when she awoke.

Suddenly one of the machines next to the bed started beeping and people were everywhere around him. *What was going on*? He had seen enough hospital dramas to know that the stationary line on the monitor wasn't a good thing. Instead of hearing the people around him their voices turned to white noise drowning out any words. The doctors and nurses were pouring through the door and pushed him to the back of the room. It was like an out of body experience watching something he couldn't quite believe. He watched a doctor take a baby's body out from under the bed covers and pass it to a nurse who laid it down on a table and was joined by another doctor. The whirring of the machine continued, and he watched his wife's body jump up, then down, over and over. It felt like his breath had been taken from him when they finally stepped away from the bed and the doctor looked to the clock as he had just four minutes ago, and then pull the sheet over her face. 'Time of Death. 23.59,' said a doctor.

Next to him the nurse and doctor were still stood by the body of his child massaging its tiny little chest. The nurse shook her head and the baby lay there motionless. Nothing. Silence. Nobody made a sound and all that could be heard was the clock. Tick tock tick tock.

Then there was a sound. A sound that pumped air back into his lungs. A noise so beautiful that the Senator's face flushed with blood, bright pink and warm. The noise of a child crying. The doctors and nurses looked at each other. It was a miracle. The nurse swaddled the child and handed it to the Senator. 'You have a baby boy sir.'

He held the boy close and knelt beside Logan. Logan's comic fell to the floor and he was beaming from ear to ear. 'Brother?' he said, and the senator laid the baby into Logan's arms. 'Mummy?'

'Mummy had to go to heaven so that we could have this beautiful little boy,' said Nathanial holding back the tears. 'Mummy wanted us to have this special little man so that I could have two amazing sons and that you could have a brother,' he looked over to the bed where she lay.

The doctor and nurse who had helped deliver the baby had remained in the room but everyone else had vacated the hospital room, presumably to move onto the next emergency. The door slammed open and a nurse ran in with a look halfway between amazement and bewilderment. 'Doctor, we need you to come and see something in the Oncology ward. They're better. The cancer has just disappeared,' she shouted.

'Who? What do you mean nurse? Which patient?' said the doctor trying to calm her down.

'All of them. They're all better.'

CHAPTER SEVENTEEN

'I recognize this chemical,' said the Professor sniffing the air.

'What do you mean?' said Logan.

'Back when Wanikiy and I were trying developmental drugs to try and cure Leukemia we were using a substance called arsenic trioxide. A poison which worked against the body but helped to rid it of the harmful diseases.'

'So, this is a cure or a poison?' Logan said still unaware of what the Professor was telling him.

'Both my friend. But what I don't understand is that the amount we are talking about here mixed into the water systems you are talking about would have absolutely no effect on anyone. It would dilute itself to nothing. To have any effect on a human being you'd need a ridiculous amount of this chemical to even have the slightest effect. Wanikiy must have known this.'

Logan looked puzzled 'So the toxin isn't a toxin.'

'I mean, yes, it is poisonous in its undiluted form and could quite easily kill a person, but if you mixed it with the volume of water you are talking about then no, it couldn't harm a fly,' said Professor Brittle.

'Sola dosis facie venom,' said Mendez

'Correct Isaac. As Paracelsus said, '*the dose makes the poison*,' quoted the Professor.

'Logan, you need to see this,' said Chuck walking through the door and switching on a TV in the lab.

Logan was watching Tallulah in his father's communications room 'She doesn't know,' he said.

'Know what?' said Chuck.

'It's not a toxin, it's a placebo. We need to get a message to her and to

Danny. We need to get him out of there now. He's in danger. Get me the satellite phone, quickly Chuck. Professor, how do we get hold of the base? Tallulah needs to know that her father isn't trying to kill anyone. But we cannot alert Goldsmith. Wanikiy and Tallulah could be in serious trouble if he finds out Wanikiy has tricked him,' said Logan.

'Logan,' Chuck said pointing at the TV.

Tallulah had the test tube to her lips and was drinking the arsenic trioxide. He looked at the Professor.

'That's going to be a problem,' he nodded.

'It'll kill her. How do we stop her? You have an antidote?' Logan said.

'There is no antidote,' said the Professor. 'Wait. Yes, perhaps something, but we need to get it to the base as soon as possible. Activated Charcoal absorbs the chemicals and might just work if we get there in time.'

'How long have we got?' said Chuck

'A few hours if we're lucky,' he replied.

'Chuck, let the others know what is going on. You have this Charcoal?' Logan said.

'Yes, I believe so,' said the Professor.

'Mendez, I need a plane, now.'

'Planes I have, pilots, not so much,' repeated Mendez.

Logan paced the room 'We're wasting time. You've got no-one?'

'Hod was the only one,' Mendez said shaking his head.

'I can fly a plane,' everyone looked around to see Xander stood at the door.

'You? How?' said Chuck.

'I used to go up in my dad's Cessna when I was four. He'd let me take the controls,' said Xander.

'When you were four?' said Chuck shaking his head in disbelief.

'Yeah, these things stick. What have we got to lose?' Xander said sucking on newly acquired rollup.

'You are loco Ese,' said Mendez 'I like him,' he approved to the others.

'We've got nothing to lose, but Tallulah has everything to lose. Let's go,' said Logan.

The group started walking, then jogging and eventually sprinting towards where the planes were. 'Chuck, I need you to stay behind. Fill in the others if they don't already know. Keep trying Danny. We need to get word to him, but don't tell him about Tallulah. We'll get word to you when everyone is safe.' Logan put his hand on Chuck's shoulder 'Thank you.'

'What else was I going to do?' Chuck smiled.

'Right,' said Logan as they got to the gates.

'This one,' said Mendez pointing to a light aircraft 'that's as close to a Cessna as I got.'

'It's great,' said Xander.

Logan opened the door of the plane and went to help Professor Brittle on 'I'm sorry Logan, this is as far as we go together,' he said.

'What?' said Logan 'I need you. Tallulah needs you.'

'No,' he replied, putting a bag into Logan's hand 'my place is here. The Government that wanted me dead put me here and this is my home. Give Tallulah the Charcoal,' he placed the bag into his hand.

Logan nodded 'Thank you, for everything,' he embraced the Professor. 'The truth will come out.'

Logan looked at Mendez and smiled 'I'll never judge a book by its cover ever again.'

'I should hope not Amigo. Stay safe. I hope we meet again someday.'

Logan and Xander got into the cockpit of the plane and Xander turned the key. The engine started turning over and the propellers started to turn.

'Still got it,' Xander smiled.

Back at the communications room Tallulah had just swallowed the toxin. She sat down at the desk awaiting what she expected to be imminent death, but still smiling into the camera. She felt an acidic taste in her throat and closed her eyes. She started to cough, and her head felt heavy. She had accepted that this was her destiny and that by sacrificing herself she would at least be saving thousands of others, that her father had condemned.

For a minute she thought the banging was in her head, but then she looked up at the door and there were two soldiers stood outside hammering on the glass windows, glaring at her. Goldsmith had joined them, smiling, presumably because he knew she wouldn't be a problem for much longer. Her father was also with him. He looked terrified and was mouthing the words 'No,' at her. She leaned back in the chair, her face warm and starting to prickle. Her eyes were watering, and she heard more banging but louder.

'This is your fault you idiot. You couldn't keep that brat under control for more than ten minutes,' said Goldsmith. 'You two go back to your stations,' he said to the soldiers. 'We will deal with this.'

'I was a bit busy trying to create a poison for you,' Wanikiy snarled.

'Get her out of there you fool,' Goldsmith barked at Wanikiy.

'It's not what you think' screeched Wanikiy through the window.

Goldsmith shoulder barged the door and as they entered the room Tallulah was passed out in the chair 'Switch that off,' Goldsmith pointed at the camera and stood with one hand on his hip and the other on his head.

'Now what?' he said out loud to himself 'It's fine. The toxin should be at the reservoir within the hour. No-one would have seen that little cow. We're all good.'

Wanikiy was knelt on the floor next to Tallulah, when The President came through the door.

'What's going on? I saw her on the monitor. Is she ok?' said President Mathers.

'She's tried to ruin the one chance we had of actually living to a decent age,' said Goldsmith.

Mathers knelt by Wanikiy 'Is she alive?'

'Barely,' said Wanikiy 'We need to get her to the infirmary.'

'Here let me help you,' the two men followed by Goldsmith carried Tallulah's limp body to the infirmary.

Only one other person was in there and that was Jay, head bandaged and looking towards the men coming towards him. He obviously knew of the plan and also that Goldsmith was involved in trying to have the rescue group impeded. He didn't know just how deep Wanikiy and President Mathers were in too. Did they know about Goldsmith's plan to kill Danny and the others? Goldsmith locked eyes with him and a knowing look that frightened Jay to the bone.

'Is she ok?' said Jay.

'No son, she's taken something very poisonous,' said the President. 'Can we do anything Wanikiy? Is there any kind of antidote to this toxin?'

'Activated Charcoal, but we don't have any on the base. She is dying,' said Wanikiy cradling his dying daughter in his arms.

Goldsmith was looking out the infirmary window deep in thought.

'It's not what you think,' he said quietly.

'What Goldsmith,' said the President.

'It's not what you think. You said that right Wanikiy? Back at the communications room. You said through the door 'it's not what you think'. What did you mean?' said Goldsmith rubbing his chin.

'I don't know what you mean,' said Wanikiy.

'Oh, I think you do,' said Goldsmith.

A soldier appeared at the door and waited before he could enter. The President waved him in 'What is it?' he said.

'We've caught sight on the external monitors of a light aircraft about one to two hours away heading in this direction. The board have insisted that you join them in the boardroom to discuss what's going on and how to deal with it,' said the soldier.

'OK, I'm coming.' He put a hand on Wanikiy's shoulder 'I'm sorry my friend. It shouldn't have gone down like this. Not at the expense of our children. We should have trusted them with the truth. I'm going to have to answer to the board and explain what has been going on. I'm so so sorry.' President Mathers left the room.

'You're not telling me something Wanikiy and I will find out what it is,' said Goldsmith pointing at him and following the President.

****

In the war room the government members sat waiting for the President around the table. The Commander General stood at the head of the table, where the President would normally sit, when President Mathers walked through the door followed by Goldsmith.

'I believe that's my chair General,' he said, 'please take a seat,' and he held out his hand to the seat next to his. 'I owe you all an explanation.'

The room was silent, and everyone paused to hear exactly what was going on outside of the walls of the underground community.

'So, I know that you have heard rumors. Rumors that some of the younger members of our community had left the base and attempted to stop the operation to poison the water supply to the outside cities. This much is true,' said the President. This drew gasps from many of the people in the room and muttering among those who held higher ranks. 'You may have also heard that these kids are being led by my son Logan and helped by Danny. This is also true.'

Goldsmith balked at this comment, bearing in mind he had known about Logan's plan long before The President had known and had attempted to stop them at any cost, even death. 'And what exactly was this plan of theirs?' said Goldsmith, already knowing the answer and knowing that the President didn't know the full extent of the group's involvement.

'All we know at this point is that a group led by Logan has gone off base to stop the operation. We can only assume that they have headed to the reservoir to stop our troops delivering the toxin. We cannot be sure if they are still alive at this time. We've had no communication with our military to confirm that they have made contact. All I can tell you is that Tallulah Wanikiy was part of this group. She returned to the base and has used our communications to the outside world to warn them not to drink the water,' he replied.

'Why would they do this? She has to be punished,' said Franklin J Pitkin.

'At this time, she has ingested some of the poison and has been moved to the infirmary. We have no idea if she will come through and we do not have the necessary medical supplies to help. With regards to punishment of her or any of these children, including my sons, we need to understand why they have done this and what they have done. All of us, in this room put into place a plan to kill off half of the remaining population to save ourselves. Each one of you voted unanimously for this to happen based on the findings of two men. We took this decision upon ourselves and we neglected to share this information with the rest of the base, which included the children. We thought that what we were doing was right, but it wasn't, and this should have been a democratic decision across the whole base as to whether we should go ahead.'

'Who are children to decide what is right and what is wrong?' said the General 'They have no life skills and no knowledge of the outside world.'

'But they are still a part of THIS world, whether above ground or below and they should have been allowed to put across their input, before we sat around a table and decided their future in less than an hour. You Franklin, Linda, Goldsmith, everyone in this room decided in less than 10 minutes that people should die so that we might live and based on what?' said the

President, leaving those last three words hanging in the air like a bad smell.

President Mathers stood and walked halfway around the room to where Goldsmith sat arms cross like a petulant child who had just been scolded. 'If this operation doesn't happen then we will die Nathaniel. It is that simple. If this band of humanitarians have stopped this happening, you may as well start digging a six-foot hole for yourself.'

'How do you know they haven't stopped it?' said the President.

'Don't be preposterous,' said Goldsmith moving uncomfortably in his seat.

'What if I told you that the operation has already been foiled?' he said putting his hand on Goldsmith's shoulder.

'How? Never? That's a lie. If that's true we're as good as all dead,' Goldsmith said.

'What if I told you that I stopped the operation from happening before it even started. What if I told you that I conspired with Wanikiy to make a toxin so deadly that it would poison someone within hours, but when mixed with high volume of water it would be like dropping a grain of sand on a beach?' said the President.

'If what you're saying is true,' said the general 'You're talking about treason.'

The room was filled with noise from everyone talking over each other, arguing and on the verge of pandemonium. Then a clap of thunder pounded down on the table and the noise stopped as quickly as it had started.

'Do you know what this is?' said The President, everyone looking at the large wad of papers he had brought down on the table. A second clap came along with another large file of what looked like data print outs. 'Or this?' Everyone was shaking their heads waiting for more to come.

'I know what it is,' said a voice from the corner of the room.

'Stand up please,' said The President. 'Tell us your name please?'

'My name is Martin. Martin Miller.

'And what do you do Martin? Here on the base. What is your role here?'

'Since The Cure I have worked on The Census Project,' said Martin.

'Can you elaborate Martin. Tell us a little more about exactly what The Census Project is?'

'Since The Cure started the government knew that there would be some kind of consequence, but obviously didn't know what the upshot would be, hence being unable to provide sufficient food to sustain the country and the wider world. Whilst they didn't know the impact it would have on the food supplies they did know that there would be an impact to the population and a subsequent increase. More so, they overlooked the fact we wouldn't be able to feed those additional people and decided to focus more on the cost of keeping those people. For example, housing and pension provisions. So, they set up The Census Project. There were hundreds of us at first, keeping tabs on the increase of the population, and then the subsequent decline when supplies ran out. Now there is just me working in a windowless room underground with limited but very accurate technology. This tells me almost within a thousand as to how many people are left in the United States.'

'Thank you, Martin, take a minute please,' said The President, still stood by Goldsmith. 'Martin, do you recognize these files on the table?'

'Yes Sir. I recognize them very much Sir. In fact, I put together those files over the past year.'

'What does it say in those papers Martin?' the President said narrowing down to his point.

'Sir, they state exactly how many people, at this point in time are still alive in our country. It also indicates the rate at which the population is dying and cross references with your geographical team, economics team and food security team on this here base.'

'So essentially this is the information that we used to base our decision to start poisoning our fellow man out there above ground?' said The President.

'Well yes and no Sir,' said Miller.

'How so Martin? Surely it is cut and dry that in order to survive these people must die.'

'Well, it's certainly a possibility,' he paused 'but in all honesty I've spent years and years working on this very scenario with a number of the best scientific brains across all of the government teams at our disposal and I can without doubt say that if one thing is true about what you've just said it's that the data is inconclusive,' Miller took a deep breath.

'Inconclusive?'

'Yes Sir. I mean, it might help, but who the Hell really knows?' said Miller looking around the room.

'So, us,' The President pointed around the room 'The government. The people in charge. The people voted into a position of trust to do what is best for the country. We, decided to dispose of human beings, based on a lie and didn't even think twice to question why,' he held his hands up. 'Guilty as charged. Treason? Hell yes. I sentenced people to death, and I did it within 10 minutes,' he shook his head. 'But,' he held up a finger 'but it didn't sit right with me. I saw my son sitting in his room alone that night thinking. He didn't see me, but I stood there looking at him and I knew something was wrong, that we had made a grave error of judgement. I was voted into this Presidency to try and clean up the mistakes made by my predecessor and here I was making one bad decision after another. So, I looked deeper, I found Martin,' he nodded. 'Wanikiy and I came up with the plan to use a placebo instead of a deadly toxin.'

'Why use any kind of plan? Why not just bring us back to the table and let us meet Mr. Miller? Surely based on his findings we all would have agreed that the plan was misguided,' said Pitkin.

'Well, this brings me to my next point. Having spoken to Martin we realized that despite the inconclusive nature of his research that there was a faction within this room that wanted the plan to go ahead regardless of the results. Martin had provided this information directly to someone within this room who had doctored the paperwork for their own agenda. Someone who believed that murder was the only option available regardless of the impact to men, women, children who had suffered already.' The President now had both hands-on Goldsmith's shoulders and Goldsmith was sweating profusely through his suit.

'Martin, one last question, who did you give your findings too?'

'Sir, that would be the Commander General.'

The General jumped up from his chair, but two soldiers had already pinned him back down into it.

'This is absurd,' he stammered.

'General Roderick. We've known for some time that you had the data and that you and a few members of your close team of military support, which are now also in custody, had this agenda planned. We knew that you would manipulate the weakest member of the board, with the most influence, to put forward the plan to poison the population. Sorry Goldsmith, they used you too I'm afraid. Had it come from the General himself he knew it wouldn't get passed without an enquiry due to his position on the military fleet. However, coming from a man of figures and on the board of directors with Wanikiy's backing there was only ever one outcome. Thankfully Wanikiy doesn't have very much good to speak of you and therefore when I put it to him to question the plan he didn't have to think too hard about it. We only let the plan go on for as long as it did because we needed to pick out everyone involved.' said The President. 'General, one question though. Why? When Martin gave you the information you must have known then that it was inconclusive and that by killing half the population it could have absolutely no impact on the current situation.'

'Are you really that stupid?' said the Commander General. 'It was a power play. You were getting nowhere. You are leading us all to our deaths down here. You're weak. The plan was meant to put the people down here at ease and give them hope. Something they've never seen before under you as leader,' he hissed.

'Hope' said the President perplexed. 'Hope is something we have always had down here. Now hope is something we can have up there too. Take him away.' The soldiers picked the Commander General out of his chair and marched him in handcuffs out of the room. 'Let's bring our kids home,' he said and walked out the room.

The General was in cuffs and would be sentenced along with his men for the part he had played in the potential genocidal catastrophe.

Running down the base corridors Wanikiy was searching for something, anything, to help Tallulah. He turned a corner and came face to face with the Commander General and his escort.

'The hypocrite himself,' said the General stopping suddenly, and bringing the soldiers to a halt.

Wanikiy tried to compose himself 'How so General?'

'Look around you, you fool. This. All this was down to you? You single-handedly brought the world to its knees. What does it feel like to be the man who destroyed the planet?'

'Destroyed it? I tried to save it, but men like you, all you see is greed and how you can exploit people. I may have created the trigger, but you and your government pulled it,' said Wanikiy.

'Come on now Wanikiy. Like there wasn't a small part of you that knew what you were doing was wrong. Disease is part of our makeup. It's the fail safe to ensure the planet keeps on turning. You just had to interfere and now look at us.'

'A fail safe?' he shook his head 'You have obviously never seen a child diagnosed with Cancer. Their body ravaged not only by the disease but by the poisons we inject to kill that disease. It not only affects them, but it affects their whole family, their friends. You have obviously never watched a loved one wither away in front of you, not knowing who you are and suffering in unimaginable pain. We needed cures, we needed to stand up to these horrible diseases that don't discriminate against anyone, good or bad, young or old. Every single person that ever worked to help get rid of these diseases is a hero. This was never God's plan. Disease is the work of the Devil and you took something that was good and turned it into evil.'

The General stood back shocked out the outburst 'HaHaHa, he laughed hysterically. Very good. Very passionate. But here we are, and if indeed I am evil then surely, I have won. The world is in turmoil and what is left of its inhabitants will likely be dead within months.'

'Maybe you have General, but as long as there is life in me then I won't give up on these people and those people out there.'

The General sneered at Wanikiy and nodded to the soldiers. It was time to move on.

CHAPTER EIGHTEEN

'We can't just wait here and hope everything is alright,' said Chuck to the others.

'We've come this, far right?' said Scott

'Oscar,' said Chuck, 'you got anything other than planes to get us back in one piece?'

'I've got just the thing in the prison garage,' said Mendez.

As Mendez opened the door to the garage he grinned 'If you thought the planes were good.' As the door swung open so did the boy's jaws. The garage contained cars that they had never seen before other than in books. 'You're loving me now, right?' laughed Mendez.

Chuck had his hand on his head.

'Baggsy the Ferrari,' said Seth, who had never driven anything other than a tractor before.

Meanwhile the others were all climbing into various sports cars.

'Whatever you want, it's yours,' said Mendez.

Chuck shook Mendez' hand and then embraced him, tears in his eyes. 'We will be back,' he said.

'I should hope so,' said Mendez 'We've got a world to fix.'

Seth looked up from the Lamborghini he was sat in, donning sunglasses he'd found on the dash 'Let's do this.' He revved the engine. Then stalled.

Mendez lifted the shutters to the garage workshop and the sun shone onto the silver rims of the cars blinding him. 'Good Luck,' he whispered to himself and watched them drive away back to their home.

****

Back at the base, the President hadn't finished with the General Commander and he caught up to him with the military police hauling him towards the base lockups. He was unrepentant and sneered when the President caught his eye.

'You're weak Nathanial. I thought you were better than this,' he said.

'Weak? I called you out, though didn't I. What were you thinking?'

'I was thinking about the country I love. It's called Patriotism,' he replied.

'That country no longer exists. We aren't at war with the people above ground. We're in this with those people. We should have integrated a long time ago. All you have achieved in doing is making me open my eyes to what we should be doing. Sharing the knowledge we already have with the people outside of this base,' said the President.

'You're a fool Nathanial. So, the data was inconclusive. It doesn't mean what we did was wrong.'

'What you did was wrong on so many levels I don't know where to start. You talk about patriotism and then try to kill half of the population. You're no better than a terrorist,' he said.

'You've sentenced the people on this base to death. How long before our secret base isn't so secret when you start spreading your word to the outside world. You and I both know what is out there lurking. We've seen it. Murder, cannibalism, death is waiting for you to come knocking on the front door,' said the General.

'You sound like you're scared General.'

'You're damn right I'm scared. It's the end of the world. But I don't think you've noticed. Now, if you don't mind Nathanial, I have places I need to be,' he smiled.

The guards around the General turned and pointed their guns at the President.

'You may have underestimated my reach Mr. President. It seems like these patriots also want to live,' said the General. 'Now if you wouldn't mind stepping into that cell.' He pushed the President backwards and slammed the door shut.

'You won't get away with this,' shouted the President.

'I already have,' retorted the General.

He turned to his men and the guards 'Are the charges set?'

'Yes General,' one of the men said.

'Good. Is this everyone?' he said counting the remainder of his army.

'I believe so,' said the same man, stepping up to the General's right side.

'A fierce and brave set of men if I do say so myself. Are you ready to make America proud again?'

'Sir, yes sir,' came the reply from the men.

'Gather as much food as you can carry and load it along with the weapons into the Humvees. We move out in 15 minutes. Set the charges. After that you are either in those Humvees or you're dead. Understood?'

'Sir, yes Sir.'

'Goodbye Mr. President, it's been a blast,' he smiled through the vent in the cell door.

The General headed off with half the men whilst the others set about the stores and carrying what they could to the transport area. No-one questioned what they were doing because they were still dressed as military guards. Within minutes the cars were loaded and ready to move out.

The general stood back away from the window of the boardroom out of view watching Goldsmith talking to himself.

'Ah, what a shame our partnership has come to an end Goldsmith. Your stupidity was your downfall, but your salesmanship was of great benefit,' he said quietly.

'Would you like us to dispose of him Sir?' said his new Lieutenant.

He thought for a moment 'No, let's see if cockroaches do survive,' he said.

****

As Xander bought the Cessna to a halt Logan was wondering how he would get back onto the base without being noticed. As it was, when he got to the entrance it couldn't have been easier. The main ramp was down, and people were running past him in blind panic, too busy to even notice him.

'Xander, follow these people. Find out what has happened. Most of all keep safe. Something's kicking off and we want to be on the right side of it,' said Logan.

'And you?' said Xander.

'I'm going in. I've got to find her before it's too late. If it isn't already.'

He shook Xander's hand and pushed past the people coming towards him running into the base.

Gunshots rang around his head and he wondered who was attacking them. This wasn't the time though. He needed to get to the communications room straightaway. He covered his head and started running in the direction of the communications rooms, where he thought Tallulah still was.

When he got there the room was empty. '*The infirmary*' he thought to himself and turned, heading back along the corridor. 'Soldier,' a woman's voice came from behind him. 'You need to get out of here. The whole place is coming down.'

'I need to get to the infirmary,' said Logan

'It's a suicide mission. This place could go at any point,' said the woman.

'I don't have a choice,' he said looking down at the activated charcoal in his hand, and he ran off.

'I know,' she said, as he ran past.

Turning back to look at the woman, Logan shouted 'Where you headed, exit is back this way.'

'To the cells,' said Rose.

Logan reached the infirmary and Tallulah was lying in bed, limp and grey. He burst through the door and Wanikiy looked up from where his head lay in her hand on the bed.

'Am I too late?' he said.

'She needs an antidote for the toxin,' said Wanikiy. 'We don't have any on the base.'

'Activated charcoal,' said Logan out of breath and holding out the bag.

Wanikiy leapt to his feet, taking the bag and mixing some of the powder with water in and pouring it between her lips. Nothing. No movement. 'More,' he said and made up another batch, forcing her mouth apart to swallow down the medicine.

Both Logan and Wanikiy stared at Tallulah urging her to move, but nothing. Then a twitch. First her finger, then her hand. 'Tallulah,' said Logan. Her eyes slowly prized apart and she blinked. 'Logan?' she spoke.

He grabbed her up in his arms. 'You're alive,' he said.

'Well, if you don't crush me, I am,' she smiled.

'We need to get out of here. Something's going on. The whole base is evacuating,' said Logan.

'It's the Commander General. Two soldiers came by about half hour ago to take Jay out, but I couldn't leave her. The whole plan to release the toxin was a ruse. The Commander General was behind it, but your father and I had to go through with it to flush him out. He's escaped and plotting to destroy the base. He's planted explosives everywhere,' said Wanikiy.

Logan looked at Wanikiy and then Tallulah. 'Thank Wakan Tanka you got here in time Logan,' said Wanikiy.

****

The President had been banging on the cell door in the hope someone would hear him and let him out. Then, just when he didn't have anything left in him and his voice had become hoarse from shouting so hard, he heard a voice on the other side of the door.

'Mr President is that you?' came the voice.

'Yes, let me out. The General has escaped and locked me in here,' he replied.

The bolt on the door clanked as the person on the other side unlocked it.

'Thank you,' he said walking through the door. 'I know you?' he said.

'Rose,' she replied.

He nodded, having never seen her in his life before.

'Do you believe in fate?' she said.

'I do now,' he replied. 'We need to get word to the rest of the base that the General and his men are still in the base and that they are planning to blow it up. They are in army fatigues and were headed for the loading bay.'

'So, just put it out on the speaker system?' she said pointing to a phone on the wall. 'That covers the stores, sleeping areas and the loading bay I believe.'

'What about the infirmary?' he said.

'No, I don't think so Mr. President,' said Rose, knowing full well Logan was heading there.

'OK, I need to get there. Put out a message on the speakers and get off the base as soon as you can,' he said. 'Oh, and thank you, Rose,' he smiled.

Rose picked up the phone and started speaking 'If you are hearing this message the Commander General has escaped from custody and has planted explosives on the base. Please evacuate immediately. All remaining military personnel proceed carefully to the loading bay. The general and his men are armed and dangerous.' Then she was gone.

The general's men had already set off the charges but hearing the message they turned their weapons on all and anyone left in the area. People were running for cover wherever possible, hiding behind anything they could. Bullets rebounded around people's heads as the men provided cover for the approaching General. 'Pull out,' he commanded as the Humvees sped out of the loading bay and up the ramp.

The base was complete panic with people grabbing what they could and jumping into trucks being driven by the remaining loyal soldiers. There were people screaming and running everywhere in the loading dock holding their worldly possessions in just one hand and their loved ones in the other. Soldiers directed them onto the transport and when the last person was on one of the army captains shouted, 'All Clear,' and the truck started its engine.

'Wait, wait,' came a voice. It was Rose.

'Ma'am, you need to vacate this area,' said the captain, just as an explosion somewhere in the building went off. 'Holy Shhh,' he said ducking.

'It's the President,' said Rose. 'He's still in the building.'

'Smith,' he shouted to one of the other soldiers 'Get this lady out of here. The President is still inside. I'm waiting.'

'Yes Sir,' said the soldier, helping Rose onto the truck.

****

Meanwhile, amongst the sounds on explosions, Goldsmith sat alone at the boardroom table his head in his hands going over the events that had just happened. He had conflicting emotions of relief that he had not been caught up in the deception of the Commander General, but also the embarrassment that he had been duped into playing an important part of the General's wicked plan. Not to mention the fact that the President was unaware he had put the children's lives at stake and sent McGregor after Danny. His rage began to boil over and he was aiming it at all the wrong people.

In his mind he felt Wanikiy should have told him of the President's plan and he should have been in the know about the General's wrongdoing from the outset. Yes, Wanikiy and his daughter were the reason that he was feeling this way. He had been made to look stupid and Goldsmith did not like this feeling at all. He stood straight up, sniffed and removed a revolver from inside his jacket. He checked it was loaded and set off to find Wanikiy.

When Goldsmith got to the infirmary, he looked through the window and to his astonishment he saw Logan and Wanikiy sat around the bed and Tallulah sat upright smiling at them. *'What the Hell. How was she alive?'* he thought to himself. More of Wanikiy's trickery and deceit no doubt.

The infirmary was the furthest point from the loading bay, with no comms unit, and they looked unaware of what was going on.

He puffed up his chest, hid the gun in his pocket and walked into the room smiling 'Tallulah my dear, so good to see you up and about. I just wanted to come and check you were alright and apologize for the way I acted in the Communications Room. I'm sure your father has filled both yourself and Logan in on the excitement. I, of course, had no idea, or I wouldn't have acted the way I did,' he turned his head towards Logan. 'Dear boy, so good to see you back safe and sound. You must have had a right time of it out there,' he waved his hand around for effect.

Of course, no-one was pleased to see Goldsmith, and he took offence at this 'Come now, I knew nothing about this plan of the General's. I was acting in the best interest of the country, as I'm sure you thought you were too,' he said. 'I've come here to apologize, and I would like us to move forward together and let bygones be bygones.'

Tallulah looked at her father and Logan with a bitter taste in her mouth from Goldsmith's words. The plan that he had put into action had resulted in the death of two of her closest friends, and although the General had orchestrated it, she held Goldsmith equally responsible.

'I suppose you know nothing about planting a mole in our team or the whereabouts of my brother?' Logan said to Goldsmith.

'As far as I am aware the troops sent to distribute the poison have been updated and recalled from the reservoir. As for a mole, it sounds like the boy was acting on his own,' replied Goldsmith.

'Yes, of course. We shall see what Danny has to say when he returns,' said Logan 'Is there anything else you wanted? We need to get off this base,' said Logan.

'No, no. I just wanted to pass on my apologies for the things out of my control,' he said.

Goldsmith turned his back on them and started walking towards the door, then stopped. He could have easily left them to die in the carnage of the oncoming annihilation of the base but instead he felt for the gun in his hand and swung back around lifting it towards Wanikiy.

'What are you doing Goldsmith?' said Logan

'Isn't it obvious,' said Goldsmith 'I'm doing what I should have done myself years ago. I mean you do know that your father is responsible for everything. The Cure was his fault. His ego is the reason that we are all living down here under the ground and why everyone else is dead.'

'Goldsmith, you know as well as I do both Brittle and myself weren't responsible that day. We were given no choice,' said Wanikiy.

'We all have a choice. You chose to go down that path and get into bed with the government. You knew as well as everyone involved that there were risks and here we are.'

'Yes, Goldsmith, here we are. I would do anything to go back and make a different choice, but that ship has sailed. All I can do now is try and do the right thing and try to be a better father,' said Wanikiy.

'I'm afraid old friend that ship has also sailed. You embarrassed me and you know I can't let that go. It seems that your decisions have yet again led you down a rabbit hole, but this time one you will not be returning from,' he turned to Logan and Tallulah 'unfortunately you two have become loose ends and we all know what happens to those,' he chuckled.

As he took aim at Logan, Wanikiy launched himself towards Goldsmith who in turn swung round and faced Wanikiy. The sound of a single gunshot rung out and both men fell into a heap on the floor. Logan stood still and waited to see any movement from either man, but both lay dormant. Then Goldsmith's long thin hand appeared and pushed Wanikiy's body off him and onto the hard floor of the infirmary. Goldsmith clambered to his feet with the gun still in his hand and smiling 'No happy ever after ending here Logan,' he said. He raised the gun again towards Logan then stopped. Goldsmith coughed and then his face started to contort and stiffen. He looked down towards Wanikiy, who had rolled over onto his back, and then looked at a syringe sticking out of his leg with the plunger compressed. He started convulsing and foaming from the mouth, the gun plummeting to the floor and then he fell to his knees before finally plunging headfirst into the ground before him. He was dead.

Logan rushed to Wanikiy who was bleeding from his chest. Logan looked for something to stem the bleeding and pushed bandage after bandage against the wound, but the bleeding continued. He shouted for help, but no-one was around. Tallulah moved from her bed to his side and they both looked at Wanikiy imploring that he knew what to do. He did. He knew that this was his time and that he would soon be with the love of his life again. 'Take care of her,' he smiled and closed his eyes. Tallulah held him and Logan placed a hand on her shoulder as she cried.

Wanikiy had died a hero, saving them and killing Goldsmith in the process.

Tallulah did not have time to grieve as an explosion sounded just outside the room 'We got to evacuate now Tals. The whole place is going up.' Logan jumped to his feet and pulled Tallulah away from her father 'Tals?' he said.

'I know,' she said pulling on a coat over her hospital gown 'Let's go.'

Halfway down the corridor the President turned the corner and almost ran straight into them. Logan beamed, 'You're alive.'

The President covered his mouth, exultant to see his son, but the reunion celebrations were short-lived as the ceiling started to collapse.

'The General has escaped.' he said.

'We know, we're leaving now. Is everyone safe?' Logan replied.

'Yes, follow me. You're the last ones. Everyone has packed what they can, and we've salvaged as much supplies as we can, but the base has been compromised. We're moving above ground.'

They started down the corridor either side of Tallulah helping her along. At the exit the Captain was still waiting for them. 'Sir, we've evacuated everyone. We have managed to get a lot of the food supplies out, along with minimal transport and weapons. We have moved the rest of the community to half a mile outside of the town.'

'Good good,' he said, 'You have any transport left?'

'Yes Sir,' he pointed to a Jeep

'Help us get her to it before the whole place blows,' said Logan.

Once in the jeep the soldier started it up and sped up the ramp, spiraling out into the town, which was also starting to crumble. They started heading to where the rest of the community had now gathered. Explosions were going off underneath them and the top surface of the base was starting to cave in leaving holes in the ground in front and behind them.

'Drive!' said Logan as the soldier dodged the openings in front of him.

Logan looked behind the car as the chasms joined each other becoming craters. In seconds they watched the remains of the base and the town falling into the charred ruins of where they had spent most of their lives.

The jeep sped towards the convergence of families from the base, who they could see were now shouting for them to drive faster, as the ravine chased them. Getting closer and closer those same people started to move as the jeep was coming straight towards them. The soldier put the brakes on seconds before reaching them and skidded to a stop, the huge gaping crater stopping only yards behind them.

They looked at each other and breathed a sigh of relief.

CHAPTER NINETEEN

By now the Commander General and his team had put enough ground between him and the newly destroyed base that he had no concerns of the others following him, either through fear, or the strength in depth he still had with his men. His supplies were primarily weapons and he knew that at some point he would need to find further food supplies to fuel the troops.

Although his plan had not worked, his ego still saw this as a win. He had overthrown the President and unaware whether he was still alive or not took comfort in the destruction of the base. He was a leader, not a follower and one more day spent underground was another day closer to death as far as he was concerned.

He looked around at his men, then at the plume of white smoke rising in the distance where the town once stood and the base underneath and smiled to himself. He felt more alive than any time in the last decade and knew that as a survivor he was safer out here than back there. He planned to recruit. He knew what was above ground and he knew the dangers it would possess to anyone still alive from the almost unarmed community. But he wasn't scared. His men were mercenaries, and woe behold anyone who came up against them.

He walked over to his Lieutenant who was hunched over a table reading a map.

'Nearest city is Texas Sir.' said his Lieutenant.

'Do we have an estimated population?' said the General.

'Sir, no Sir. Miller's data wasn't clear on actual figures. Only projected,' he replied.

'Seems a lot of his data was inconclusive,' said the General, once again trying to justify his actions. 'We head through Texas, picking up anyone who could be an asset. We're building an army Lieutenant.'

****

'Yes, yes, I understand,' said Hod as he put down the satellite phone to Logan.

He tried to pull himself up onto the wing of the plane and after several attempts succeeded. On the side of the plane near the cockpit was a few rungs which led to the roof of the plane. He climbed up and on top of the small plane was small seat in front of a very large machine gun. Hod, picked up his binoculars and looked out into the distance where he saw a convoy of military vehicles heading his way. The Commander General sat back in the first jeep in full military outfit with the sun shining off his medals smiling, looking directly back at Hod through his own binoculars.

Hod aimed the machine gun towards the jeeps and locked it into place 'Here we go,' he said.

****

One Hour Later

'No sign of the Dwarf Sir,' said the Lieutenant to the Commander General.

'Miles and miles of desert with no-where to hide and you can't find one man, albeit it a very small one,' said the General.

'Sir, no Sir. Shall we continue to look?' replied the Lieutenant.

'No, prepare the men for battle.'

'Sir, yes Sir. Are we going back to the base camp?' said the Lieutenant.

'No. We're heading to Parchman, Mississippi.'

CHAPTER TWENTY

Later that night when the events of the past week had been discussed and discussed and discussed again, the President walked away from the other leaders and over to the group of kids who were waiting patiently to find out their punishment. Chuck, Seth and Scott who had returned from the prison were being filled in on what happened with the Commander General.

'So, what's the verdict pops?' Logan said to his father.

'I'm afraid we have no option other than to banish you from the community. You're on your own.' The group gasped.

Then, breaking into a smile laughing they realized he was joking.

'Dad,' said Logan punching him on the arm.

'Things have changed massively. We've lost our home, we've lost our supplies, we've lost most of our security force and I must take most of the blame for that. Although the decision I made was the right one, the decision not to tell everyone was the wrong one. We weeded out the bad eggs but at a cost to our way of life. It's going to take time to rebuild and it won't be easy. The board will remain in place, but I'll no longer be President. I'll be an equal on the board with an equal vote on what happens. Also, we want you to be on the board too Logan. You guys have a voice and you've shown that it is as important as anyone's. What do you say Logan?'

'No,' replied Logan curtly. 'You need someone who will motivate, who will empathize and more than anything give their life for their friends and family.' He pointed to Tallulah. 'Only one person fits that bill.'

Nathaniel nodded. 'Good choice,' he said smiling at Tallulah, and the group starting clapping. Tallulah blushed and held her hands together in thanks.

'Now what Mr. Pres... Mr. Mathers?' Chuck stammered.

'Now we get some sleep and tomorrow decide our next move. I don't think the Commander General will come back for us, but we can't be sure. We need to find a new home as well. Out here we're sitting ducks and that's where you guys come in. You know more about up here than any of us. Our lives are in your hands.'

'Safe hands,' said Xander lighting up a cigarette.

The President walked away back to the base camp, which had now been set up resembling a small shanti town. Life would never be the same and he knew that they would face new challenges, especially now they had lost the security they once took for granted. The decisions over the past week had weighed heavily on him. He missed his confidante Wanikiy who he always knew he could rely on for sound advice. So many lives lost and was it even worth it? Could he have done it someway different. Now he would never know.

The rest of the group sat back down in front of a campfire they had built.

'So,' said Jay. 'You're telling me that the toxin wasn't actually a toxin?'

'No, it was a toxin. It just wasn't strong enough to do what the Commander General thought it would do? Logan's dad and Wanikiy had set up the whole thing to extract the Commander General as a traitor,' said Scott.

'So,' said Jay, again. 'You're telling me that our whole plan was actually for nothing? And McGregor attacked me for no reason? And you travelled miles and miles to find a professor who may or may not have been alive, on the chance he may or may not be able to create an antidote to the toxin, that wasn't really a toxin? Danny went to the reservoir to destroy it when it didn't need to be destroyed and is now missing, presumed dead.'

'Well when you put it like that. Erm, yes. I suppose we did,' said Seth.

'We lost Brad Junior and Faye simply because of a lack of communication and trust. Tallulah could've died too. I could have died. People need to see the bigger picture. The world is in turmoil and it's moments like this more than ever that we need to support each other,' said Jay, the rest of them nodding.

'Oh, and one last thing,' he said. 'Who in the holy hell of this whole mess is Rose? And where did she go.' Everybody shrugged.

$$* * * * * * * * * * * * * *$$

As he did before everything had transpired, Logan sat alone with his head in his hands looking out to the darkness of the vast desert.

'Penny for your thoughts,' said Tallulah as she put a hand on his shoulder and sat down beside him.

'Jay's right you know. Brad, Faye and Danny are dead because of me.'

'You know that's not true. You had a choice and you made the right one. They made a choice too. To follow you because you spoke the truth. Your passion for other people makes you a natural born leader. They didn't die for nothing. They died for a cause,' she said.

'I miss him,' he replied. 'He was my brother and I sent him out there to die, knowing it was always going to be a possibility.'

'I know. I do too,' said Tallulah 'He was my friend too. But we still have each other and together we have a future. We know we can make this work. It won't be easy, but we can do this. I love you.'

As they reflected, they heard shouting coming from over by the fire.

'What's that noise?' said Chuck. Everyone shushed each other listening.

'Maybe it's the General, coming back to attack,' Seth said jumping up to attention.

'No, listen. It sounds like'.

'A motorbike,' said Logan.

Epilogue

'I remember my father telling me bedtime stories when I was a young girl, of a time where people lived their lives carefree and happy'.

'Those days are long gone now and just weeks after the collapse of the community the days have become harder and harder. Lack of food and water has meant rationing, and now fuel reserves have depleted we travel by foot across barren land scavenging whatever we can. Families have left the community to go it alone. Some returning to the destroyed sight of the base to see if they can live within in the rubble and find any supplies.

With less than 800 of us left we don't know if we can even make it to the closest city.

Fighting among the remaining base community is commonplace and the board members have disbanded with no hope of survival in the coming days.

Our own group, who once took on the government, continue to fight the good fight but knowing what waits for us in the cities scares us more than knowing the Commander General could return at any time to kill us all. Some even pray for death.

Logan and his father try to lead us but even they are losing hope. We are slowly turning into animals.

We have now lost all contact with the Prison, Professor Brittle and Mendez. No-one is coming to save us. We are alone.'

The Cure

<u>ACKNOWLEDGEMENTS</u>

Thank you to my long-suffering wife Toyah for pushing me to write this book and realize my dream of publishing something someone, somewhere, may wish to one day pick up and read. Thank you to my beating heart; Joshua, Jacob and Bethany. My purpose in life and the people who save my soul daily. Thank you to my mum, Sandra Horgan, who I don't thank enough for what she does for me. Now it's in print so if I ever forget please turn to this page and repeat. I really am grateful. Thank you to Juju, my Grandma, Julia Horgan B.E.M. who bankrolls me on a weekly basis and feeds the cats. Thank you to Stuart Craig for all your support and help with the kids. It never goes unnoticed and is appreciated. Thank you to all my friends over the years who have always been there for me. Your loyalty and respect are worth more than all the dollars in the world.

Thank you also to Lynette Anderson for her publishing advice. Thank you to Danial Evans for your continued support with this project. Thank you to Darren Bowen for showing me that stepping outside your comfort zone reaps rewards.

Finally, thank you to all the doctors and nursing staff of Piam Brown Ward, Southampton and Poole Hospital for looking after my boy. Martin Hussey, you are a legend. Thank you.

COMING SOON

<u>PARCHMAN</u>

47365534R00094

Printed in Poland
by Amazon Fulfillment
Poland Sp. z o.o., Wrocław